QWERTY STEVENS
BACK IN TIME
THE EDISON MYSTERY

Dan Gutman

Aladdin Paperbacks
New York London Toronto Sydney Singapore

Thanks to Douglas Tarr of the Edison National Historic Site, West Orange, New Jersey. At the Smithsonian, Hal Wallace and David Burgevin provided valuable help.

Photos courtesy of the U.S. Department of the Interior, National Park Service, Edison National Historic Site.

This book is a work of fiction. Any references to historical events, real people, or real locales are used fictitiously. Other names, characters, places, and incidents are the product of the author's imagination, and any resemblance to actual events or locales or persons, living or dead, is entirely coincidental.

First Aladdin Paperbacks edition December 2002
Text copyright © 2001 by Dan Gutman

ALADDIN PAPERBACKS
An imprint of Simon & Schuster Children's Publishing Division
1230 Avenue of the Americas, New York, NY 10020

Also available in a Simon & Schuster Books for Young Readers hardcover edition.
Designed by Paula Winicur
The text of this book was set in Sabon.

Printed in the United States of America
4 6 8 10 9 7 5 3

For my mom, of course!

Everything in this book is true,
except for the stuff I made up.*

There is a secret dark room, upstairs in the labora-
tory building, where only two chosen assistants are
permitted to work with the master. Doubtless there
are fabulous goings-on in that room.
—Matthew Josephson, Edison: A Biography

I have been at work for some time building an
apparatus to see if it is possible for personalities
which have left this earth to communicate with us. If
this is ever accomplished, it will be accomplished, not
by any occult, mysterious, or weird means . . . but by
scientific methods. . . . There are two or three kinds of
apparatus which should make communication very
easy. I am engaged in the construction of one such
apparatus now, and I hope to be able to finish it
before very many months pass.
—from the personal diaries of Thomas Alva Edison

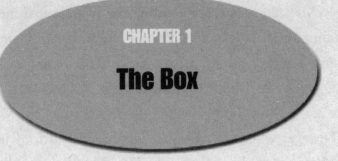

CHAPTER 1

The Box

Qwerty Stevens found the box at four o'clock in the afternoon on October 18. He would always remember the date because it was the day after his thirteenth birthday.

He found the box right after he'd had another one of those arguments with his mother. *She* said he had gone over to Joey Dvorak's house without getting permission first. *He* said he had asked for permission. She said "maybe" did not mean "yes."

He said, she said. The next thing anybody knew, Qwerty's mother was saying that he was grounded.

Mrs. Stevens wasn't mean. She just *seemed* mean sometimes. It was hard for her, bringing up Qwerty and his two sisters all by herself. Six years earlier Qwerty's dad had been killed in a car accident. He was driving home on Franklin Avenue in West Orange when a teenager lost control of a Jeep Cherokee and plowed right into Mr. Stevens's little Honda. He was killed instantly. The teenager walked away with a few bruises.

"Robert Edward Stevens!" Mrs. Stevens called out in her firmest voice. "Don't you *ever* go *anywhere* without getting my permission first, do you understand me?"

Mrs. Stevens called him by his real name only when she was mad. And she used all *three* names only when she was *really* mad. The rest of the time, she called him "Qwerty," like everyone else.

He had gotten that nickname when he was in third grade. The whole class was in the computer room practicing keyboarding one day. The computer teacher told the class to put their fingers on the keyboard and type—without looking—the top row, left hand (QWERT), then the top row, right hand (YUIOP). Then they were instructed to type the middle row, left hand (ASDFG), and the middle row, right hand (HJKL;). Then they had to move their fingers down and type the bottom row, left hand (ZXCVB), and the bottom row, right hand (NM,./). Then they had to print out their work and turn it in.

Robert Stevens had a problem lining up the paper in his printer. Somehow he clipped off his name from the top of the page. When the computer teacher was going through everyone's papers, she held up Robert's to show what happened when you didn't load the paper into the printer correctly. This was what the top line said:

```
Name: QWERTY
```

From that moment on, everybody had called Robert Edward Stevens "Qwerty."

Qwerty slammed the back door on his way out. *Mom's just being overprotective,* he thought. *I'm*

thirteen now. I'm old enough to go over to my friend's house by myself. She's just afraid the same thing that happened to Dad will happen to me.

When Qwerty was mad, or when he was in a bad mood, he liked to dig. He'd take a shovel out of the garage and go to a corner of the backyard where the grass never grew. Then he would dig a hole. He never had a goal in mind. He just liked to dig holes. He found it relaxing.

Qwerty never dug up anything good. One day he found a rock in the shape of a triangle that looked like it could have been an old Indian arrowhead. More likely, it was just a rock in the shape of a triangle.

While he was digging, nobody ever bothered him. He didn't think about anything.

Mrs. Stevens figured digging gave Qwerty an outlet for his anger. And to be honest, it kept him out of her hair for a little while.

It was while he was digging that Qwerty found the box.

The ground was well worn. He had dug holes out in the backyard many times before. *Maybe if I dig*

deep enough, he thought, *I can climb in and nobody will ever bother me.*

Qwerty pointed the shovel at the earth and placed his right foot on top of it. He leaned in, and the blade sliced into the dirt. And then, less than a foot below the surface, something stopped the blade from going any farther.

Thunk. A definite *thunk.* It wasn't a *clank,* which would have told Qwerty he had hit something made of metal. No, it was definitely a *thunk.*

Qwerty pulled up the shovel and placed it a few inches to the left of the mark he'd just made. He leaned on it again, just enough to cut through the soil without damaging anything that might be down there.

Thunk. There was something down there. It didn't feel like a rock.

He placed the shovel a few inches to the right of his original mark. When he leaned on it—very carefully—he felt something stop the shovel and heard the *thunk* noise again. Whatever was down there had to be at least a foot wide.

Qwerty got down on his knees and began to loosen the dirt with his hands. It came away easily. In a few minutes he had cleared off enough dirt so he could touch the top of whatever was down there. It felt like it was made of wood.

"Whatcha doin', Qwerty?"

Qwerty looked up quickly. He had been concentrating so hard on digging that he hadn't noticed anyone standing there. It was Thing One and Thing Two—his sisters.

Madison, the little one, was six. She was curious but harmless. Barbara, the bigger one, was sixteen and nosy and had achieved her full potential to be annoying.

Qwerty didn't say anything about what he was doing. Whatever was buried down there, he didn't want to share it with them.

"Nothin'," he lied.

"Whoso diggeth a pit shall falleth therein," Barbara recited dramatically.

"Nobody asked you, Barb."

Barbara had recently discovered a love of poetry,

which made her more annoying than ever.

"It's a free country, Nerdy. Ever hear of freedom of speech?"

"Aren't you going to get in trouble for digging up the backyard?" Madison asked.

"I never have before. And besides, trouble is my middle name," Qwerty replied, getting up and clapping the dirt off his hands.

"No, it's not," Madison said. "Your middle name is Edward."

"Come on, silly," Barbara said as she took Madison by the hand. "The only thing dumber than digging holes in the ground is watching somebody *else* dig holes in the ground."

When Thing One and Thing Two were out of sight, Qwerty got back down on his knees. He pushed the shovel all around the hole he had made and figured out that the object had to be a rectangle about two feet wide and one foot long—about the size of a backpack. He couldn't tell yet how tall it was.

Dirt was packed around the thing pretty tightly,

and Qwerty was having a hard time getting it out. There was no handle or anything on top to grab on to. He scraped more dirt around the sides and tried to rock the thing back and forth. Dirt was getting under his fingernails, and his hands were filthy. He knew his mother would get on his case about that, but then, what else was new?

Finally Qwerty removed enough dirt on all four sides to free the thing from its grave. He lifted it out of the ground.

It was a wooden box with a curved top, sort of like one of those carriers people used for bringing their cats to the vet. It wasn't too heavy. Qwerty could lift it easily. There was a small lock on one side. Part of the wood was rotted away. This thing, whatever it was, had been buried in the backyard for a *long* time.

Dirt was still caked on the sides of the box. Qwerty brushed it off with his hand, revealing these letters in flowing gold:

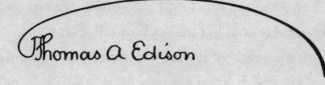

CHAPTER 2

Some Kinda Machine

Seeing the name of the world's most famous inventor on a wooden box buried in the backyard did not come as a *total* shock to Qwerty Stevens. For the second half of his life Thomas Edison had lived and worked in West Orange, New Jersey. Edison's old laboratory, now the Edison National Historic Site, was right on Main Street in West Orange. His mansion, Glenmont, had been—and still was—half a mile up the road in a section of town called Llewellyn Park.

Qwerty Stevens lived in Llewellyn Park, in one of the much smaller houses bordering Edison's mansion.

Qwerty's father and grandfather had grown up in the same house.

Edison's mansion and laboratory were open to the public, but in his whole life Qwerty had never been to either. Somehow things close to home didn't seem quite as interesting as if they were in another state or a different country.

As soon as he dug up the box, Qwerty brought it inside and called his friend Joey Dvorak. Joey loved old stuff. The walls of his room were covered with antique posters and advertisements. Every Saturday he went from yard sale to yard sale, looking through other people's junk to add to his collection.

Qwerty, on the other hand, loved *new* stuff. Computers, audio-video gear, digital doodads, state-of-the-art anything. His room was filled with so much of this junk, it was hard to see the floor. His mother was constantly telling him to clean up his room.

"Dja get that scanner you wanted for your birthday?" Joey asked when he recognized Qwerty's voice on the phone.

"Yeah," Qwerty said, "but I've got something

even *cooler* to show you. It's right up your alley. Come on over."

"I'm there."

Joey ran over to Qwerty's house and went up to his room without bothering to knock. He was tall and lanky, and he towered over Qwerty.

"Lock the door," Qwerty instructed him, lowering his voice so his nosy sisters wouldn't hear.

"This must be really good," Joey whispered excitedly.

"It is."

Qwerty opened his closet door and took out the wooden box. He brought it over to his desk, clearing some stuff out of the way to make room.

"It's an antique Edison phonograph!" marveled Joey.

"How do you know?"

"I can tell by the box. That's the case Edison phonographs came in during the late 1800s. It's probably worth hundreds of dollars. Open it up."

"I don't have a key," Qwerty said.

"Bust the lock," Joey suggested.

"Won't that make it worth less money?"

"The wood is all rotted anyway," Joey pointed out. "Just break it."

Qwerty took a screwdriver from his desk drawer and fiddled with the lock. It wouldn't open, but he slid the screwdriver behind the lock and was able to pry it away from the wood. The lock clattered to the floor.

Together Qwerty and Joey lifted the lid and peered inside.

"It's not a phonograph," Joey said immediately.

"What is it?"

"I don't know. Some kinda machine."

"Well, duh . . ."

Together the two boys lifted the machine out of the box and put the box out of the way on Qwerty's bed. Lowering the machine back onto Qwerty's desk, the boys put their faces right up to it, examining it carefully. There was a complicated jumble of delicate wires going every which way. It appeared as though the wires were connected to a series of magnets, but it was hard to tell for sure.

When they looked closely, they could also see several crystals, a tiny motor, and a grayish substance that neither of them could identify. There was a wire coming out of the back of the machine, but no plug.

"It's a beautiful old thing," Joey said, shaking his head. "But I have no idea what it is."

While Qwerty fished a magnifying glass out of his desk drawer, Joey looked in the wooden box to see if there might be a clue inside.

There was. A piece of paper. Joey tapped Qwerty on the shoulder and unfolded the paper wordlessly. They read it together:

From the Laboratory
of
Thomas A. Edison,
Orange, N.J.

The world is not ready for this.
I'm not sure it ever will be.

October 1879

CHAPTER 3
Edison's Mystery

Qwerty and Joey looked at each other with wonder, both of them doing arithmetic in their head. The machine Qwerty dug up in the backyard had been buried out there for . . . more than 120 years!

"This . . . is big," Joey said slowly.

"Think of it," Qwerty marveled. "Thomas Edison was the most famous inventor ever. The guy invented the phonograph. He invented the electric light. He invented motion pictures. He got patents for over a thousand inventions in his lifetime—"

"But," Joey interrupted, "he decided not to tell

anybody about this *one* invention. Why? You think it was a failure?"

"Nah. If it were a failure, he would have just trashed the thing. He took the trouble to bury it out in his backyard and put this note with it."

"Maybe we should bring it to the Edison National Historic Site," Joey suggested. "Maybe one of the researchers there can tell us more about it."

"And maybe one of the researchers will take it away from us and claim it's government property," Qwerty scoffed.

"We could bring it to school and show it around."

"So some kid can drop it and break it?" Qwerty snorted. "No way."

"We could sell it and make millions," Joey said, his eyes lighting up at the thought.

"Maybe," agreed Qwerty. "But first I think we should try and see what it does. Edison thought the world wasn't ready for this machine in 1879. Maybe the world is ready for it *now*."

There was a sudden knock at the door. Qwerty quickly picked up the machine. Joey opened the closet door, and they slid the machine into the closet on top of Qwerty's board games. Qwerty grabbed one of his video-game magazines and flipped another one to Joey. The boys tried to look casual as Qwerty opened the door.

"Mommy says to wash your hands for dinner," Madison squeaked. "How about teaching me how to use your computer tonight, Qwerty?"

"No," Qwerty said brusquely.

"Why not?"

"You're not old enough. You'll break it."

"Will not!" Madison whined in a voice that meant she might just decide to cry if she didn't get her way.

"Okay, okay! I promise I'll show you how to use the computer . . . someday."

"So what were you digging up in the backyard before?" Madison asked Qwerty. "That hole was pretty deep."

"Nothin'," Qwerty replied, glancing at Joey.

"Buried treasure?" Madison asked.

"You might say that."

He didn't want to tell Madison the truth, partly

because he wanted to keep it a secret and partly because she was kind of a pest and he didn't like her nosing around his stuff.

"Why don't you go play with your dolls?" Qwerty suggested.

Madison wrinkled up her nose, squinted her eyes, and burst into tears. "Mom!" she cried. "Qwerty's being a sexist pig again!"

Joey decided that was his cue to leave. But before he could go, Qwerty grabbed him by the elbow.

"This is our secret, right?" Qwerty whispered. "Let's keep it between you and me."

"You, me, and Edison," Joey agreed. They shook on it.

Dinner was tense. Madison was mad at Qwerty because he wouldn't teach her how to use his computer. Barbara was mad because some boy at school had snatched her notebook away and read one of her poems out loud in front of their entire English literature class. And their mom was mad because, well, because she had to work all day and then come home to cook dinner for three bratty kids but no husband. At least that was the way it seemed sometimes to Qwerty.

Nobody spoke much at dinner except Madison, who complained about all the mean things Qwerty had said to her lately.

"You know what parents do with tattlers?" Qwerty asked, putting his face close to Madison's. "They put them up for adoption."

"I don't wanna be 'dopted!" Madison sobbed, and ran out of the kitchen in tears.

"Robert Stevens," Qwerty's mother said wearily, "you can go to your room for that."

Barbara threw Qwerty a smirk.

"What did I do?" Qwerty asked.

"Go to your room *now*."

"You're always picking on me. I didn't do any-thing."

"Go *away*!"

"Maybe I should just go away *forever*," Qwerty mumbled as he pushed his chair from the table and threw down his napkin. He didn't mean it, but he'd wanted to say something really mean and that was the first thing that came to his mind.

Qwerty stormed upstairs, making sure to pound each step as loudly as possible. He stayed in his room all night, reading his magazines and listening to CDs.

Before he went to sleep, he pulled the mysterious Edison invention out of the closet and looked at it one more time.

CHAPTER 4

Poof!

"I hope all of you are working on your reports for International Day," Mrs. Vaughn announced as the students filed into her history class the following morning. "They're due next week."

Mrs. Vaughn told the class to take their seats and put their things away. The seventh grade at Thomas Edison Middle School was finishing up a unit on the history of New Jersey. Mrs. Vaughn challenged the students to name famous Americans from their home state. Hands shot into the air.

"Frank Sinatra!"

"Bruce Springsteen!"

"Jack Nicholson!"

"John Travolta!"

"Meryl Streep!"

"Derek Jeter!"

"Who's Derek Jeter?" Mrs. Vaughn asked. The kids all laughed.

"He's a famous baseball player!" a few kids yelled, happy to tell their teacher something she didn't know.

"Can anybody name a famous New Jerseyan who isn't an entertainer or athlete?" asked Mrs. Vaughn.

"Grover Cleveland!" somebody hollered.

"That's right. He was our twenty-second president. Any others?"

Qwerty raised his hand.

"Thomas Edison," he announced.

"Good. Edison wasn't *born* in New Jersey," Mrs. Vaughn informed the class. "He was born in Ohio. But he lived in New Jersey most of his life. And I'm sure most of you know that he created many of his inventions right up the street at his laboratory. Does anybody know how many inventions

Thomas Edison made in his lifetime?"

"A hundred?" one of the boys in the back row volunteered.

"A million?" said a girl up front.

"One thousand ninety-three," said Mrs. Vaughn.

The class let out a big "Wow!" Joey Dvorak scribbled something on a slip of paper. He folded it up, passed it to the girl next to him, and motioned for her to pass it to Qwerty. When it reached Qwerty, he unfolded the paper and read it:

$$1,094!$$

Qwerty looked over at Joey, who threw him a wink.

After school Joey and Qwerty walked home together. They had homework to do, but the mysterious machine in Qwerty's closet was irresistible. They had to tinker with it first.

West Orange High School let out earlier than the middle school, so Qwerty's sister Barbara was already home when Qwerty and Joey arrived. She was in Qwerty's room, fooling around at the computer.

"Out," Qwerty ordered Barbara. When it came to dealing with sisters, Qwerty's philosophy was never to use two words when one got the point across.

"Well, if it isn't Pinky and the Brain," said Barbara. "How will you attempt to take over the world this afternoon?"

Barbara and Qwerty were always more comfortable making fun of each other when their mother was out of the house. Mrs. Stevens, who was a librarian, wouldn't get out of work until five o'clock. Then she had to pick up Madison from her after-school program.

"Out," Qwerty repeated.

"It's my computer too," Barbara complained.

"Look at the calendar, Thing One."

According to the system they had worked out, Qwerty had use of the computer on Mondays and Wednesdays. Barbara had it on Tuesdays and Thursdays. Most weeks neither of them needed it on Fridays. On weekends they negotiated rights to the computer. This month the computer was in Qwerty's room. Next month they would move it to Barbara's. The system seemed to work. Barbara and Qwerty didn't fight about the computer too much, at least no more than they fought about anything else.

"Your new scanner is really cool," Barbara said. "Check this out."

There were about a dozen overlapping windows scattered around the computer screen. Qwerty was always working on so many projects at the same time, he could barely keep track of them. He liked to keep everything in front of him on the computer desktop, so all his projects would be at his fingertips.

Barbara clicked the mouse, and one window jumped in front of the others. It was the report Qwerty had been writing about Spain for International Day. The report began,

Spain is a mountainous country in southwest Europe about the size of Montana. It is cut off from the rest of Europe by the Pyrenees. Spain is bordered by France, Portugal, the Mediterranean Sea, and the Atlantic

Ocean. The capital, Madrid, is right in the middle of the country.

Barbara had found a photo of Qwerty, put it in the scanner, and electronically pasted it into the report on Spain. In the middle of the text, there was Qwerty's smiling face. She had used a drawing program to put a simulated sombrero on Qwerty's head. She'd even animated the photo, so the Qwerty figure was doing a little dance. To top it off, Barbara put flamenco music in the background. Like Qwerty, Barbara knew her way around a computer pretty well.

"Cute, huh?" Barbara complimented herself. "I saved it on the hard drive in case you want to use it for your report. I could write you a poem about Spain, if you'd like."

"No, thanks," Qwerty said. "Can we have a little privacy please?"

"That's gratitude for you," Barbara snorted as she left the room.

Qwerty locked the door behind her. He went to his closet and took out the Edison machine. Handling it like a precious jewel, he placed it on his desk in front of the computer. Both boys peered at the machine closely.

"I still can't figure out what it is," Qwerty said.

"Maybe it's some kind of primitive computer gizmo," Joey guessed.

"I doubt it," Qwerty said. "Edison died long before the computer was invented."

"Yeah, but the man was a genius," Joey said. "He was way ahead of his time. Maybe he created a modem or something. He was so frustrated he didn't have anything to plug it into that he buried it and never told anybody about it. People would have said he was crazy."

"*You're* the one who's crazy," Qwerty laughed.

Still, Qwerty couldn't come up with a better idea. He knew a lot about electrical wiring, having once rewired the whole kitchen for his mom. But the circuitry inside this machine was so complicated and confusing. In addition to the usual magnets and wires and relays, there were some things in there that Qwerty couldn't even identify.

"It must be some kind of communications device," Joey guessed. "Edison did a lot of work with the telegraph, the telephone, the phonograph, and movies."

"Whatever it is, it can't *possibly* work a whole century later," Qwerty insisted. "It probably *never* worked. That's why Edison buried it. It's just a piece of junk, I guess."

"Hey," Joey said, brightening. "Why don't you hook it up to your computer?"

"What for?"

"I don't know. To see what happens."

"I know what'll happen," Qwerty said. "Nothing."

"It couldn't hurt to try."

"It doesn't even have a plug."

"You're an electronic genius," Joey said. "Can't you *make* a plug?"

Qwerty shrugged. In his experience it was hard enough just getting *new*, out-of-the-box peripherals to work with a computer. This device was more than a hundred years old. It was incompatible . . . with everything. He didn't even have any idea what it was supposed to do.

On the other hand, though, fooling around with the machine had to be more fun than doing homework.

In his closet Qwerty kept a box full of computer cables, plugs, jacks, and other electrical odds and ends he had accumulated over the years. Most of it was useless. But he didn't like to throw anything away, because every so often a part would come in handy.

He rummaged through the box until he found a plug that fit the jack in the back of his computer and a cable that looked like it could be spliced onto the wire sticking out of the Edison machine. Using a screwdriver and razor blade, Qwerty attached the cable to the machine and plugged it into the jack on the back of the computer that was marked AUXILIARY.

"If this thing messes up my PC, it's your fault," Qwerty warned Joey.

The report on Spain, with the image of Qwerty

dancing around, was still on the screen. He moved the mouse around, clicking various buttons and menus.

"See?" Qwerty said. "Nothing happens. Told you."

"Try plugging it into the modem thingy," suggested Joey.

Qwerty shrugged and reached around the back of the computer. He removed the plug from the auxiliary port and inserted it into the modem port. He clicked around the screen again. Again, nothing happened.

"See?" Qwerty said, turning away from the computer to face Joey. "How can you expect a primitive nineteenth-century machine, put together long before the first computers were even *dreamed* of, to work with a twenty-first-century computer? It's ridiculous."

But as Qwerty spoke, a soft hum came out of the Edison machine. The hum was so quiet that neither of the boys heard it or noticed it.

After a few seconds some words began to scroll across the computer screen. Foreign words. Looking past Qwerty's shoulder, Joey noticed them. He pointed at the screen.

QUERIA DAR CLASES DE ESQUI ACUATICO.

"What does that mean?" Joey asked.

"I don't know," Qwerty replied. "It looks like Spanish."

"Is this part of your sister's little show?"

"I don't think so."

Qwerty clicked everything in sight. The words continued scrolling across the screen. LLEVAN TRES DIAS SIN RECOGER LA BASURA. He started hitting various combinations of keys to see if that did anything.

"Nothing's hap—," Qwerty said as he tapped the ENTER key.

And that was all he said. At the instant his pinky pushed down the ENTER key, Qwerty vanished from the chair on which he was sitting.

Poof! He was gone.

Joey blinked, then looked around the bedroom nervously.

"Qwerty!" he called, the panic rising in his voice. Joey was alone in the room. He got up and looked in the closet, but Qwerty wasn't in there.

"Very funny, Qwerty!"

Joey didn't know what to do. He thought about fooling with the computer himself, but he wasn't a computer person the way Qwerty was, and he was concerned that he might push the wrong button. He thought about telling Qwerty's sister, but he was afraid.

In a panic Joey quietly unlocked Qwerty's bedroom door and dashed out of the house.

CHAPTER 5

No Hablo Español

As Qwerty's pinky pushed the ENTER key on his computer, he blinked. When he opened his eyes again just one-tenth of a second later, he was standing on the sidewalk in the middle of a busy city. It was a city he had never seen before.

Qwerty looked up and saw skyscrapers towering overhead. He looked down and saw that he was standing on a brass plaque. The plaque read: KILO-METER 0.

He looked around. Between the skyscrapers were little twisting alleys jammed with older, crumbling buildings. The street was dotted with all kinds of stores, mostly outdoor cafés. People sat there sipping drinks. He couldn't understand the writing on the signs.

A beggar walked up to Qwerty. He held out his hand and jabbered something in a language that certainly wasn't English. When Qwerty didn't respond, he walked past. Businesspeople hurried by, then a man dressed in rags walking alongside a donkey. Some kids dribbled a soccer ball back and forth.

Mystified and shaking, Qwerty started walking with the crowd. A poster on the wall of a building advertised a bullfight. A little newsstand was stuffed with newspapers and magazines. Instead of the *New York Times* and the *Star-Ledger*, they displayed *La Vanguardia* and *El Pais*. A street sign at a large intersection read CALLE DE ALCALÁ.

"Buenos dias," a girl about Qwerty's age said as she passed him, sharing a giggle with her girlfriend.

That's when Qwerty Stevens figured out where he was—in Spain.

If Qwerty had boarded a 747 jet in New York City

and flown to Spain, the trip would have taken about seven hours. But somehow Thomas Edison's machine—connected to Qwerty's computer and linked with his report on Spain—had transported him thousands of miles . . . literally in the blink of an eye.

Qwerty stopped dead in his tracks. The back of his neck felt hot and sweaty. *How am I gonna explain this to Mom?* he thought. Mrs. Stevens just about pitched a fit when Qwerty went over to Joey's house without getting her permission. How would she react when she found out he had gone to *Spain*?

Of course, she never *would* find out unless he could figure out a way to get home.

Qwerty jammed a hand in his jeans pocket and came up with two crumpled dollar bills. If he could get some change and find a pay phone, maybe he could call home and somehow explain what had happened.

There was a store on the corner with boxes of fruits and vegetables in front. The sign above the store said FRUTAS DE AMERICA. Maybe the old man sweeping the sidewalk could help.

"Saludos, amigo!" the friendly-looking old man said as Qwerty approached. "Mucho gusto."

"Uh . . . buenos dias," Qwerty replied, struggling to recall the list of Spanish expressions he had included in his report. "Por favor. He perdido mi calzoncillos."

The old man looked at Qwerty with a puzzled expression on his face. "You have lost your underpants?" he asked in a thick accent.

"You speak English!" Qwerty replied happily. "No hablo español."

"A little English," the old man said proudly, holding his thumb and first finger about an inch apart. "Just enough."

"Where am I?" Qwerty asked.

"Why, the Puerta del Sol, of course!" the old man laughed. "The center of the world!"

Puerta del Sol. Qwerty remembered those words from his report. The city of Madrid was right in the middle of Spain, and the Puerta del Sol was a famous square right in the middle of Madrid. It was the spot from which all distances in Spain were measured.

So that's *why I landed on the Kilometer 0 plaque,* thought Qwerty. *The Edison machine sent me right to the midpoint of Spain.*

Qwerty didn't want the man to think he was dumb, and he didn't want him to think he was a runaway, either. "I am a tourist," he lied, "visiting Spain with my school choir. I am sorry that your country was cut off from the rest of Europe by the Pyrenees. That was not very nice of them."

"But señor, the Pyrenees, they are mountains."

"Oh," Qwerty replied simply. "I knew that." He looked at the fruits and vegetables, hoping to change the subject.

"Would you like to buy something, señor?" the old man asked, holding up what looked to be a hot dog.

"Yes, maybe," Qwerty said. "What is that?"

"Fried baby eel," the old man said. "Freshly caught."

"Uh . . . no gracias very much," Qwerty said quickly. "I'm not hungry. Can you tell me where I can change American dollars into Spanish money?"

"Si, I can do that for you."

The old man took the crumpled bills and fished coins of varying sizes out of a wooden cash box. Some of the coins had holes in the middle of them.

"The American dollar is worth one hundred and fifty pesetas this week," the old man said as he counted off the change. "Here are three hundred pesetas. One peseta equals one hundred centimos, señor."

"Gracias. Do you have a pay phone? I need to call my sister in America."

"America?" The old man chuckled to himself. "Señor, you cannot even call England for three hundred pesetas."

Qwerty's emotions, which he'd managed to hold in check since he arrived in Madrid, could not be restrained any longer. He put his head in his hands to hide his face and began to sob.

"I'm lost," he moaned. "I was home just a few minutes ago and now I'm here. How did this happen? I'll never get back. It was an accident. I just hit the ENTER key, and the next thing I knew I was in Spain.

Why do I always get into trouble?"

The old man put an arm around Qwerty's shoulder and led him inside the shop. "Here. Sit," he instructed Qwerty. "Use my telephone. No charge. Just two minutes, okay? Eat this. It will make you feel better."

He handed Qwerty a twisted, bready thing about six inches long.

"Eel?" Qwerty sniffed, holding the thing away from his face.

"Churro," the old man replied, pouring a brown liquid into a cup. "It is like a . . . doughnut. Fried in olive oil. You dip it . . . in chocolate."

Qwerty did as he was told and found the churro to be delicious. As he munched it, he told the old man his phone number. The man dialed what seemed like about a hundred numbers and then handed the receiver to Qwerty. It rang three times before Barbara picked up.

"Barb!" Qwerty yelled excitedly.

"Qwerty?" she asked. "I thought you were in your room a few minutes ago."

"I was."

"Well, where are you now?"

"I'm in Spain!" Qwerty shouted frantically. "You gotta get me home!"

"Very funny," Barbara laughed. "You know, Mom'll be home any second. You're gonna be in trouble—"

"Look, I don't have time to explain, Barb. Just do what I say. Go to my room and get on the computer."

"Oh, gee, I don't know if I can do that," Barbara said. "Today is *your* day and *I'm* not allowed to use the computer until tomorrow."

"Just *do* it!" Qwerty yelled. "I only have two minutes!"

"Okay, okay." Barbara was on the cordless phone, and she took it with her into Qwerty's room. "Now what?"

"Is my Spain report on the screen?" Qwerty asked.

"Yeah," Barbara reported.

"Good. Now click something!"

"Click what?"

"Anything!" Qwerty shouted.

While Barbara was trying everything she could on the computer, the old man tapped Qwerty on the shoulder.

"I must go make a delivery," he said. "Hang up the telephone when you are through, por favor."

"Okay," Qwerty said. "Two minutes. Gracias."

"Adiós," the old man said with a wave. "I hope you find your underpants, señor."

"Uh, yeah. Me, too. Hasta la vista."

Qwerty turned back to the receiver.

"Did a man just say he hopes you find your underpants?" Barbara asked.

"He said I hope you find your way to *France*," Qwerty lied.

"It sounded like—"

"Forget it," Qwerty said, cutting her off. "Have you tried everything?"

"Everything but the ESCAPE key," Barbara replied.

"Try that."

Barbara hit the ESCAPE key. The instant her pinky pressed the key, Qwerty vanished from the fruit stand in Madrid and reappeared in his bedroom exactly where he had been a few minutes earlier. One moment Barbara was sitting at the computer, and the next moment Qwerty was sitting there too, on her lap.

"Hey, get off!" Barbara hollered as she pushed Qwerty from her lap and onto the floor. "How did you do that?"

Qwerty looked around his messy bedroom, comforted by the familiar posters on his walls and his favorite things surrounding him. He struggled to his feet.

"You're not going to believe what I'm about to tell you," he said. "Joey and I agreed that we weren't going to tell anybody, but now I have to tell you. Remember when you saw me digging out in the yard yesterday? Well, I found a box. Inside the box was this machine."

Qwerty pointed behind the computer to show the machine to Barbara.

"It was invented by Thomas Edison in 1879. He never told anybody about it. Anyway, I hooked the thing up to my computer, and it . . . sent me to Spain."

"You're right," Barbara said. "I don't believe it."

"I'm telling you, it happened!"

"Don't be silly," Barbara laughed. "You can't just travel from one place to another without physically going there. It violates all the laws of physics."

"Then how was it," Qwerty asked, "that I was talking to you on the phone one second and sitting on your lap the next second?"

"I don't know," Barbara admitted. "It was some trick, I guess."

Qwerty reached into his front pocket and pulled out the Spanish money the old man had given him. "It was no trick," he told Barbara as he handed her the coins. "I don't care if you believe me or not. But I was in Spain."

Soon Mrs. Stevens came home from work, after picking up Madison at her after-school program. The three children busied themselves setting the table and helping their mother get dinner ready. When they finally sat down to eat, Mrs. Stevens asked—as she did every night—"So, what did everybody do today?"

"Nothing," Barbara said.

"Nothing," Madison said.

"I went to Spain," Qwerty said, and everybody laughed.

CHAPTER 6

The Anytime Anywhere Machine

When Qwerty got back from Spain, one of the first things he did was call Joey Dvorak. He figured Joey might have been a little shaken up when he disappeared before his eyes.

"Hey, I'm back," Qwerty said when Joey picked up the phone.

"What happened?!" Joey shouted. "I was spooked."

"I went to Spain, man!" Qwerty told him. "It was like a miracle. For about ten minutes I was right in the middle of Madrid."

"Cool! So the Edison machine works!"

"Like it was right out of the box."

"What did you do in Spain?"

"Well," Qwerty admitted, "mostly I freaked out and tried to call home. Barbara was the only one here. I told her what to do on the computer, and she zapped me back."

"I thought we agreed not to tell anyone about the machine," Joey said, a little hurt coming through in his voice.

"I had to," Qwerty explained. "Otherwise I would have been stuck in Spain."

"Forget it," Joey said. "Listen, there's something you should know. When I left your house, I bumped into some guy."

"What kind of guy?"

"He said he was a researcher or something for a company called Sixth Sense. He was asking questions about Thomas Edison."

"He's probably writing a book," Qwerty said. "You didn't tell him anything about the machine, did you?"

"No," Joey said. "But it was right after you disappeared, and I was nervous. I'm not a good liar. He might have been able to tell. He might come around asking you questions too."

"Don't worry about it, man," Qwerty assured him. "The guy's probably harmless."

Sure enough, the following day, while Mrs. Stevens and the children were preparing dinner, an old Volkswagen pulled up in front of their house. A man got out. Instead of ringing the front doorbell, he walked around the back and circled the yard before knocking on the back door.

"Mommy, there's a man outside!" Madison announced.

He was an odd-looking guy. Short and chunky, middle-aged, with long, crazy hair that seemed to float over his head, defying the law of gravity. His jeans had holes in the knees, and he wore a flannel shirt over a T-shirt. He held a clipboard in his hand and had a pencil behind his ear.

"I'm sorry to bother you," the man said through

the screen. "My name is Ashley Quadrel. I'm doing some research about Thomas Edison. May I have a few minutes of your time?"

This was not unusual in West Orange. There were hundreds of books and articles written about Edison. People were always trying to track down more information about the man. Mrs. Stevens ushered Quadrel inside.

"I work for the Sixth Sense Institute," Quadrel continued. "We're a paranormal think tank based nearby here in Livingston."

"Crackpot," Qwerty whispered to Barbara.

"What's a crackpot?" Madison asked.

"Shush!" said Mrs. Stevens.

"Yes," laughed Mr. Quadrel, "many people think of us as crackpots. We prefer to think of ourselves as open-minded. We investigate paranormal phenomena—life after death, time travel, ESP, things like that."

"Sounds like interesting work," Mrs. Stevens said.

"It is. In any case, Thomas Edison, as you may or may not know, was very interested in the paranormal.

Ever since he passed away in 1931, there have been rumors that Edison experimented with a mysterious invention he never patented or told the world about."

Barbara glanced at Qwerty. He shook his head quickly, as if to say, "Don't say a word."

"We at Sixth Sense believe this device could have been a transmatter machine," Mr. Quadrel continued. "That is, it could transport matter anyplace at any time. In fact, around the office we refer to it as the Anytime Anywhere Machine."

"Cool!" Madison said. "Are you selling them?"

"I wish I could," Mr. Quadrel laughed. "But the Anytime Anywhere Machine has never been found. If Edison did invent it, he must have hid it very well. We figure that if it does exist, it must be around Edison's old laboratory or home here in West Orange. That's why I'm visiting people who live here. Have you come across any old machines while working on your house, or working in the garden?"

"No," Qwerty said quickly.

"Not that I can think of," Mrs. Stevens added.

"Why are you so interested?" Barbara asked.

"Well, I'm a bit of a frustrated inventor myself, so I know a little bit about the process of invention. And if the Anytime Anywhere Machine truly existed, it would change the world! Think of it! We would be able to go to London, Hong Kong, or Mexico City instantly. Perhaps we could travel through time or bring back people who have died. Such a machine would be the ultimate shortcut. People wouldn't have to go anywhere. We could just *be* there. No more cars or trains or planes or other means of transportation. We wouldn't need them. There would be no more traffic jams. No more roads, for that matter."

Mr. Quadrel was getting worked up, thinking about the possibilities. His eyes flashed brightly as he talked. He waved his arms around.

"Edison's phonograph took what was once silence and turned it into sound," he explained excitedly. "His electric light took the darkness of night and turned it into daylight. Those inventions changed the world. *This* invention would take travel and make it immediate," Mr. Quadrel said with a snap of his fingers. "It would be the most dramatic change in civilization since the invention of the wheel. That's why we desperately want to find it. If anybody in history was ever able to create such a wonderful invention, it would make sense that the person would have to be Thomas Edison."

"I could use something like that," Mrs. Stevens said. "But I haven't seen any old machines lying around."

"Me, neither," Qwerty lied, stepping purposefully on Barbara's foot.

"Neither have I," Barbara agreed.

"I did," Madison piped up. All eyes turned to her. "I'll go get it," she said. Before anyone could say anything, Madison dashed upstairs.

Qwerty went to run after her, but Mrs. Stevens grabbed him by the elbow and instructed him to wash up for dinner.

Did Madison see the machine? Qwerty wondered. He sweated it out for about a minute, when Madison came downstairs with a shopping bag.

"Is this what you're looking for?" Madison asked. "I found it in the storage room."

She pulled out an Atari 2600, one of the first video game systems. It had once belonged to her dad, who must have stashed it in the basement years ago.

"Not exactly," Mr. Quadrel said. "Do you mind if I look around a little bit?"

"We're about to sit down to eat," Mrs. Stevens said. "Perhaps some other time."

Qwerty let out a sigh of relief and led Mr. Quadrel toward the door.

"I noticed several large holes out in your backyard as I came in," Quadrel said, looking into Qwerty's eyes. "Did you dig up anything interesting out there?"

"Yeah," Qwerty lied. "A lot of dirt."

"Well, please hold on to this," Quadrel said, handing Qwerty a business card. "If you find anything, give me a call."

After the dinner dishes were cleared away, Qwerty and Barbara just about tripped over each other in a mad dash upstairs to Qwerty's room.

"So you found Edison's secret invention?" Barbara

asked excitedly. "The Anytime Anywhere Machine?"

"That's what I was trying to tell you," Qwerty said as he locked the door.

"Where shall we go?" Barbara giggled, bouncing on Qwerty's bed.

"We?" Qwerty asked. "Who said *you* could go anywhere? *I* found it."

"Oh, come on, Qwerty. I share my stuff with *you*."

"But I don't *want* any of your stuff."

"Please?"

"Oh, all right," Qwerty agreed reluctantly.

"London . . . Paris . . . Tokyo . . . Rome," Barbara said dreamily.

"The North Pole . . . the Basketball Hall of Fame . . . Six Flags . . . ," said Qwerty. Then he got a devilish grin in his eyes.

"Hey," he said, "I know the perfect place to go."

CHAPTER 7

Test Flight

"Let's go to T and E!" Qwerty yelled.

"Shhhh!" Barbara giggled. "You're a genius!"

Treats and Eats was a state-of-the-art ice-cream parlor on Main Street in West Orange. People came to T and E from all over northern New Jersey because they had just about every flavor of ice cream and candy in the world. From floor to ceiling the store was stocked with gum, chocolate, giant lollipops, licorice, jawbreakers, flavored popcorn, and candies most people had never even heard of.

T and E even had its own Web site, so kids could

whet their appetite with a virtual tour through the store. Qwerty had always thought that if there was a heaven, it would probably be a lot like Treats and Eats.

Before embarking on an ambitious trip to Paris or London, Qwerty and Barbara agreed it would be a terrific idea to use the Anytime Anywhere Machine to make a short "test flight" over to Treats and Eats.

Besides, they were starving for something sweet. Mrs. Stevens's idea of "dessert" after dinner was sliced melon, apples, or some other disgustingly healthy snack. Qwerty, Barbara, and Madison weren't allowed to eat junk food, which made them want it that much more.

"Not a word of this to anyone," Qwerty warned Barbara.

"My lips are sealed," she assured him.

While Qwerty fiddled with the computer, Barbara ran into her room and returned with a five-dollar bill and her eleventh-grade class photo. She slipped the photo into the scanner, next to the photo of Qwerty she had used for his report on Spain.

He scanned the photo into the computer. Then he

logged on to the Treats and Eats Web site. The opening screen, a display of dancing candies, came up.

Barbara reached around the Anytime Anywhere Machine to flip the switch up, but Qwerty slapped his hand down on hers.

"Wait," he said, "If we *both* go, there'll be nobody here at the computer to bring us back home."

"Maybe Madison can bring us back," Barbara suggested.

"She's too young," Qwerty said. "She might mess it up."

"We could always walk home from T and E if we had to."

"Mom would flip if she caught us going out without her permission," Qwerty said as he deleted his photo from the scan. "You go alone. I'll stay here and bring you back in five minutes."

"Better make it ten," Barbara said. "What should I get for you?"

"Cotton candy," Qwerty said, licking his lips. "The biggest size they have."

Qwerty flipped the switch on the Anytime

Anywhere Machine and clicked his way over to the Virtual Tour section of Treats and Eats. The Anytime Anywhere Machine began to hum. A dialog box on the screen read TAKE TOUR.

"Ready for takeoff?" Qwerty asked.

"A-OK," Barbara replied.

Qwerty hit ENTER. Instantly his sister disappeared.

At the same instant, Barbara appeared in aisle 2 of Treats and Eats, nearly knocking over a display of Pez dispensers. The store was jammed with kids, and none of them seemed to notice Barbara appear out of thin air.

Barbara walked around for a minute, a wide grin on her face. Einstein and Newton were wrong, she thought. It *was* possible to go from one location to another without actually moving your body. The Anytime Anywhere Machine was the coolest invention since E-mail.

The line behind the counter was long, and it was moving slowly. Barbara quickly got into it. In about nine minutes Qwerty would be bringing her back, so she had to act fast.

"Can I cut in front of you?" she asked the boy

ahead of her in line. "I'm in a big hurry."

"Hey, I'm in a hurry too," the boy replied with a sneer. "Wait your turn like everyone else."

Barbara looked at the clock on the wall, which was made entirely of Tootsie Rolls. She wasn't sure how much time she had left, but it wasn't much. Finally it was her turn at the counter.

"Cotton candy," she said hurriedly. "The biggest you have. And a large mint-chocolate-chip sugar cone. Oh, and a small cookies-and-cream cone."

"Slow down!" the man behind the counter said soothingly. "It's only ice cream. Miss, we're sold out of cotton candy today."

"Oh." Barbara quickly tried to think of what else Qwerty liked. "Then I'll have a large watermelon cone instead."

The man went to scoop the ice cream. Barbara looked at the clock again. She had about a minute left, maybe two. She pulled the five-dollar bill from the pocket of her jeans and put it on the counter. She wished she had told Qwerty to bring her back in fifteen minutes instead of ten.

It seemed like it took forever for the man to finish making the cones. When he finally brought them to the counter, Barbara grabbed them and shoved the bill in his hand. He turned around to get change from the cash register.

Meanwhile, sitting at the computer, Qwerty decided ten minutes was up. He hit ESCAPE.

The man behind the counter at Treats and Eats turned around to give Barbara her change. But she was gone.

"That girl just . . . disappeared!" the man said.

Barbara landed roughly back on the chair in Qwerty's room, almost dropping the ice cream on his computer keyboard.

"It works!" Barbara bubbled excitedly.

"Of course it works," Qwerty said. "Where's my cotton candy?"

"They were sold out. I got you a watermelon cone instead."

"I hate watermelon ice cream," Qwerty complained.

"Sorry!" said Barbara. "I didn't have a lot of time."

"Who's the third cone for?" Qwerty asked.

"I wanted to bring back something for Madison," Barbara giggled. As Qwerty scowled and hid the Anytime Anywhere Machine under one of his dirty T-shirts, Barbara tiptoed over to Madison's room and knocked on her door. Madison scampered out and gratefully accepted the ice cream cone.

"Where'd you get these?" Madison asked, expertly licking around the cone to stop it from dripping on her hand.

"It's a secret," Barbara snickered.

Despite his protests, Qwerty reluctantly took the watermelon ice-cream cone and licked it. Claiming he didn't want to let perfectly good food go to waste, he licked it again.

All three kids were thoroughly enjoying their ice cream when there was a *tap, tap* at Qwerty's door. Qwerty and Barbara looked at each other in panic. As the door opened, they put their cones behind their backs in a pathetic attempt to hide them.

"I'm tired," Mrs. Stevens yawned. "I wanted to say good—"

"Look, Mommy!" Madison said, holding up her cone like the Statue of Liberty. "We got ice cream!"

"I see," Mrs. Stevens said, putting her hands on her hips. "And where did you get the ice cream?"

Nabbed, Qwerty and Barbara brought the cones out from behind their backs. "Uh . . . ," Qwerty searched for an excuse. "They just sort of . . . appeared."

"Appeared, huh?" Mrs. Stevens said angrily. "Well, it appears to me that all three of you are grounded for a week. How *dare* you go into town without my permission? And at night, too! Give me those cones."

"I didn't do anything!" Madison said, bursting into tears and running into her room. "It's not fair!"

"Why can't you just behave?" Mrs. Stevens scolded Qwerty and Barbara. "Except for school, you are not to leave this house for seven days."

"Can I invite Joey over?" Qwerty asked.

"No! And clean your room. It's disgusting." She slammed the door behind her.

●●●●●●●●●●

Qwerty and Barbara each took a deep breath. They had seen their mother angry, but never *that* angry.

"Seven days," Qwerty moaned, lying back on his bed. "If I have to stay in the house for seven days, I'll go *insane.*"

"Seven days is like forever," agreed Barbara.

A haze of gloom settled over the bedroom as Qwerty and Barbara resigned themselves to the fact that the house would be their prison for the next week.

But slowly, very gradually, a thought occurred to both of them. Qwerty sat up in bed and looked at Barbara. Then he looked at the Anytime Anywhere Machine, hidden under the T-shirt on his desk. Qwerty and Barbara broke out in mischievous smiles.

Maybe being grounded wouldn't be so terrible after all.

CHAPTER 8

A Message Across Time

Being grounded, Qwerty and Barbara realized, was probably the best thing that ever happened to them. They were forbidden to leave the house, but thanks to the Anytime Anywhere Machine, they could go anywhere in the world . . . at the click of a mouse.

The possibilities were staggering. As soon as their mother left the room, Qwerty took two sheets of notebook paper out of his desk drawer. He gave one to Barbara, with a pencil. They each compiled a wish list of places they'd always wanted to visit.

This was what Barbara's list read:

Paris

London

Rome

Walt Whitman's home

Tokyo

Rio de Janeiro

King Tut's tomb

This was what Qwerty's list read:

The Basketball Hall of Fame

Bill Gates's house

The North Pole

Michael Jordan's home

The locker room of the Dallas Cowboys cheerleaders

Mount Everest

Fort Knox

To prevent arguments, Qwerty and Barbara agreed on a travel schedule that would be fair to each of them. After school on Monday and Wednesday, Qwerty would get to go on a trip. Barbara would stay at the computer so she could bring Qwerty back home at a prearranged time. After school on Tuesday and Thursday it would be Barbara's turn to go on a trip and Qwerty's turn to stay at the computer. Qwerty would take a trip on Saturday, and Barbara would take one on Sunday.

That left Friday open. Barbara agreed that Qwerty deserved the extra day because he was the one who'd found the Anytime Anywhere Machine in the first place.

Both Stevens kids were satisfied with the trip schedule. Qwerty noticed that Barbara seemed to be treating him a lot nicer since they discovered the power of the Anytime Anywhere Machine. Barbara noticed that Qwerty was not his usual snotty self. For the first time since they were little kids, they had something in common—a secret.

"I was wondering," Barbara said after they had planned out a full week of trips around the world, "if the Anytime Anywhere Machine is so amazing, why did Thomas Edison want to keep it a secret?"

"I don't know," Qwerty replied. He went to his

computer and double-clicked his encyclopedia program. "Maybe we should try to find out before we go
anywhere else."

A search through the encyclopedia for "Edison,
Thomas" brought a biography of the famous inventor to the screen in seconds.

"Look," Barbara said, "it says Edison patented
one thousand ninety-three inventions in his lifetime.
He must have taken out a patent on everything he
created. Why not this? It doesn't make sense."

"The note he left with the machine had a date on it,"
Qwerty told her. "Eighteen seventy-nine. Something
must have happened that year that made him bury
the thing in his backyard."

"But what?"

Qwerty closed the encyclopedia program and
logged on to the Internet. A search for Edison's name
turned up dozens of Web sites devoted to the man and
his inventions. One of them was run by the Edison
National Historic Site, right there in West Orange.
Qwerty clicked on the address—www.nps.gov/edis—
and the computer quickly located the opening screen.

One of the features of the Edison Web site was a time line. You could click on any year in Thomas Edison's life—1847 to 1931—and read about what he was doing that year. Qwerty clicked on 1879.

Thomas Edison was thirty-two years old in 1879, the computer reported. He was already world famous, having invented the phonograph two years earlier. He spent 1879 working almost nonstop on his most famous invention, the electric light. The Web site didn't say anything about the Anytime Anywhere Machine. It certainly didn't mention that Edison secretly buried anything in his backyard.

It was getting late. Qwerty and Barbara decided to continue their detective work the next day.

Before going to sleep, Qwerty carefully moved the Anytime Anywhere Machine to the floor behind his desk. He put an old poster on top of it. With all his other junk scattered around, nobody would ever notice the Anytime Anywhere Machine. The last thing he wanted was for his nosy little sister to come in and start messing with it.

●●●●●●●●●●

Qwerty had a hard time sleeping. He couldn't stop thinking of all the places he was going to visit that week. He could hardly wait.

Somewhere around six o'clock in the morning a quiet hum came out of the Anytime Anywhere Machine. A soft beeping noise came out of the computer. Qwerty punched his pillow a few times and buried his face in it, trying to sleep.

But the beeping continued. It sounded like one of Qwerty's old electronic toys. A few of them, when their batteries started to run down, would beep and sometimes even *talk* in the middle of the night even though they hadn't been turned on. It was a little creepy.

But this was a different noise, Qwerty realized. It was a regular, repeating pattern of beeps. It sounded like a code or something.

Qwerty got out of bed. The beeps sounded like they were coming from his computer. His screen saver was on—an army of flying toasters slowly moving across the screen. Qwerty touched the mouse, and the screen saver left the screen. The Edison Web site was still up.

At the bottom of the screen were a series of dots and dashes. The computer made a soft beep every time it displayed a dot and a longer beep every time a dash came on the screen.

•▬ •••• ▬▬▬ ▬•▬▬

Qwerty recognized the dots and dashes as Morse code, which he'd learned about in school. It was a simple language that was used by ships and telegraphers a long time ago.

•▬ •••• ▬▬▬ ▬•▬▬

He didn't understand Morse code, but he went to his bookshelf and rifled through the pages of a few of his science books until he found it.

Matching the dots and dashes on his computer screen with the code in the book, Qwerty was able to decipher the message: "AHOY . . . AHOY."

Ahoy? The first thing that came to Qwerty's mind was Chips Ahoy cookies. Couldn't be that. Then he

INTERNATIONAL MORSE CODE

A	·—	1	·————
B	—···	2	··———
C	—·—·	3	···——
D	—··	4	····—
E	·	5	·····
F	··—·	6	—····
G	——·	7	——···
H	····	8	———··
I	··	9	————·
J	·———	0	—————
K	—·—		
L	·—··		
M	——		
N	—·		
O	———		
P	·——·		
Q	——·—		
R	·—·		
S	···		
T	—		
U	··—		
V	···—		
W	·——		
X	—··—		
Y	—·——		
Z	——··		

PERIOD	·—·—·—
COMMA	——··——
INTERROGATION	··——··
COLON	———···
SEMICOLON	—·—·—·
HYPHEN	—····—
SLASH	—··—·
QUOTATION MARKS	·—··—·

remembered that *ahoy* was a nautical term. People on passing ships greeted one another by saying "ahoy" instead of "hello."

"*AHOY*," Qwerty tapped out in Morse code, using the period and hyphen keys on the keyboard. Very quickly a different pattern of dots and dashes appeared on the screen.

•▬▬ •••• ▬▬▬ •• ••• ▬ •••• • •▬•• •

Qwerty grabbed a pencil and paper and rushed to translate the code. It said, "WHO IS THERE."

"*QWERTY STEVENS*," Qwerty tapped. "*WHO IS THERE?*"

▬ •••• ▬▬▬ ▬▬ •▬ ••• •▬ • ▬•• •• ••• ▬▬▬ ▬•

Qwerty figured it out: "THOMAS A EDISON."

Qwerty laughed. He had spent a lot of time chatting on-line with people all over the country. Sometimes boys would pretend they were girls. Or girls would pretend they were boys. Or kids would pretend they were grown-ups. In cyberspace nobody ever knew who was really who.

Qwerty tapped, "*LOL*," which is computer shorthand for "laughing out loud." Then he tapped, "*WHAT IS YOUR REAL NAME?*"

"THOMAS A EDISON," repeated the beeps from the other end.

Qwerty decided to play along. "*WHAT YEAR IS IT, TOM?*" he tapped.

".■■■■ ■■■.. ■■... ■■■■." was the response.

Qwerty gulped. *1879!* How could this prankster know that he had been trying to find out what Thomas Edison was doing in 1879? Could it be a coincidence? As he was puzzling it out, the computer started beeping again.

"IS IT STILL THE 19TH CENTURY?" was the coded message.

"*NO*," Qwerty tapped, "*THE 21ST.*"

"MY GOD!" was the return message. "IT WORKS!"

Qwerty didn't believe for one minute that the person he was chatting with was the real Thomas Edison. Edison had been dead for over seventy years. Clearly, it had to be some imposter playing a practical joke.

Then again, Qwerty had used the Anytime Anywhere Machine to send himself to Spain and back home again. Barbara had used it to go to Treats and Eats. The machine *worked*. Who was to say that Thomas Edison couldn't make it work to communicate across two centuries?

Edison—or whoever it was—next sent a message saying he was tapping out his part of the conversation on a telegraph key he had hooked up to his latest invention. Qwerty asked him to describe the machine, and a description came back almost immediately.

Qwerty looked under his desk. The machine Edison described was *identical* to the machine he had dug up in the backyard.

"*YOU REALLY ARE THOMAS EDISON, AREN'T YOU?*" Qwerty tapped, incredulous.

"COME HERE," appeared on Qwerty's screen in Morse code. "MERGENY."

"*WHERE?*" Qwerty tapped.

"MY LAB. WST ORANG, NEW JERS."

"*I LIVE IN W.O.*," Qwerty tapped.

"GOOD," Edison replied. "WON'T HAVE FAR TO GO."

"*WHAT IS EMER?*" Qwerty asked.

"CANT SAY," Edison tapped. "OTHER MAY E ISTENING. COM NOW. N PERSO."

Qwerty noticed that at first Edison's words were spelled correctly, but as they chatted, more and more letters were missing. The beeping signal seemed to be breaking up.

"*HOW?*" Qwerty asked.

"FIG OUT WAY," Edison replied. "IMPORT. NEED YOU BRING SOMETH."

"*BRING WHAT?*" Qwerty tapped quickly.

There was no response. The beeping stopped. The transmission was over.

CHAPTER 9

Meet the Wizard

As soon as the message from Edison stopped, Qwerty took off his pajamas and pulled on his jeans, a T-shirt, and sneakers. Instinctively, he grabbed his backpack from his chair and slung it over his shoulder.

He flicked on the scanner next to his computer and scanned in the photo of himself. The Edison Web site was still on the screen, with the time line set at 1879.

For a moment Qwerty thought about knocking on Barb's door and telling her what he was doing. But he knew she would go ballistic if he woke her up before her alarm clock went off. Instead he took a piece of crumpled scrap paper and wrote "*HIT ESCAPE KEY*" on it. He slipped the paper under Barbara's door. If he went away, Qwerty figured, Barb could bring him back home.

Qwerty went back to his desk and sat down at the computer. Hesitantly, he hit the ENTER key.

He vanished.

"Out of the way, you imbecile!" a man yelled.

Qwerty dodged to the left, narrowly avoiding getting whacked in the head by a long wooden plank.

He looked around and saw that he was in a large, long room that appeared to be some sort of machine shop. There were lots of men hurrying around, some of them as young as Qwerty. Others were stationed at tables, pounding hammers against metal, grinding handsaws into wood, or working with wires and bottles. No women were in sight.

Various machines were whirring and chattering. Steam was hissing. It was so noisy Qwerty had to cover his ears. Flies buzzed around like they owned the place. There was no air conditioning, and the heat was almost unbearable. The smell of chemicals and sweat filled Qwerty's nostrils. He wrinkled up his nose with disgust.

Shelves covered the walls from floor to ceiling, filled with tools, microscopes, Bunsen burners, oddly shaped glass containers, magnifying glasses, and hundreds of chemical bottles. Only after taking this all in did Qwerty spot the sign on the far wall: THOMAS A. EDISON, INCORPORATED.

He had done it, Qwerty realized! Not only could Edison's machine send him to Spain, it could also send him to Edison!

A door opened and a man strode into the room. He didn't look like Thomas Edison. At least, he didn't look anything like the photos Qwerty had seen of Edison. This man was much younger. He was handsome, about five feet eight, with soft, straight dark hair that was starting to turn gray. It flopped down over his forehead, and he brushed it back with his hand.

From the way he walked into the room and the

way the workers looked at him, it was obvious that the man was the great Thomas Edison himself.

If Qwerty had to sum up Edison's appearance in one word, it would have been *disheveled*. There were gray smudges on his black suit and pants. Underneath the suit he was wearing a dark vest and wrinkled white shirt. His bow tie was crooked and loosened. He carried a cigar, which he hadn't bothered to light. His posture was slightly stooped. His complexion was pale. He didn't look like he spent a lot of time outdoors.

But Edison was *alive*. He whipped around the room like a tornado, stopping to peek over the shoulder of one worker, to ask a question of the next one, and to issue an order to the next. He seemed to be working on a dozen or more projects at once.

Edison looked up and noticed Qwerty staring at him.

"You, boy," Edison barked before Qwerty could say a word, "I'm not paying you to stand there gawking. Get me four ounces of nitrous peroxide!"

Qwerty was paralyzed with fear and awe. Edison's steel blue eyes bored in on him. The eyes were bleary and tired, as if he hadn't had enough sleep, but they also seemed to crackle with energy.

Edison came over to him. Qwerty could see the man's yellowed teeth, the stubble on his chin, and the dandruff on his shoulders. Qwerty tried to speak, but his mouth couldn't seem to form words.

"Why do you fix me with that vacuous stare of incomprehensibility, young man?" Edison demanded. "Nitric acid! Is *that* within the scope of your under-standing?"

"Uh . . . where is it?" Qwerty mumbled.

Edison leaned over, cupping a hand around his right ear and placing that ear almost against Qwerty's mouth. Qwerty remembered learning in school that Edison was almost totally deaf. Qwerty also realized something they'd never taught him in school—Thomas Edison had bad breath and body odor.

"You work your articulating apparatus so weakly I can't make out a word you're saying!" Edison shouted at the boy. "Go to the supply room, you harebrained dumbbell!"

Qwerty wanted to tell Edison he wasn't one of his

employees, but Edison was already at the next table, peering into a microscope and ridiculing somebody else. Qwerty dashed off in search of the supply room.

The Edison laboratory was a huge complex of a dozen or more buildings, each one with a specific purpose. One building had a sign on it that said WOODWORKING. Another said METALLURGY. Other buildings were devoted to chemistry, photography, and research. Qwerty ran all over the complex until he saw a door marked SCRAP HEAP.

Inside it looked like the Addams Family was having a garage sale. There were hundreds of boxes and bins scattered all over the place, each one filled with some other weird thing. There were animal skins, feathers, rocks, hardware, peacock tails, and walrus tusks. Qwerty hadn't seen such a mess since . . . well, since he left his room at home.

A little bell was on the counter, and Qwerty tapped it to make it ring. A burly guy rumbled out of the back room.

"You new?" he asked.

"Uh, I guess so."

"What's that you're wearin'?"

Qwerty looked himself over for a moment before he realized the man was referring to his pants. "They're jeans."

The man looked at Qwerty's pants again. "Gene don't wear no pants like them."

"No, they're *jeans*," Qwerty explained. "Blue jeans."

"We ain't digging for gold here, son," the man grunted. "Get yourself a proper pair of black pants before you come to work tomorrow."

"Yes, sir."

"Name your poison," he said gruffly.

"Nitric acid," Qwerty replied. "Mr. Edison needs four ounces."

The man went in the back room and emerged a few minutes later with a test tube. There was liquid inside it and a cork at the top to seal it. He jotted something down on a pad of paper and had Qwerty sign his name before surrendering the test tube.

"What's this?" Qwerty asked, picking up a large, soft object behind the counter and examining it.

"A rhinoceros ear."

"What do you need *that* for?" Qwerty asked, dropping the ear quickly and wiping his hand on his pants.

"I don't," the man said. "But I know that one day the boss is gonna come in here and say he needs a rhinoceros ear for some experiment. When he does, I'll be ready."

Qwerty hurried back to the lab, where Edison and one of the workers were pouring some kind of powder from little jars into a larger one. Edison took the test tube from Qwerty without a word and poured the nitric acid into the large jar. Smoke poured out of the jar, and Edison nodded his head with approval.

Before Edison could move on to the next table, Qwerty worked up the courage to speak to him.

"Mr. Edison!" he shouted in the great inventor's ear. "It's me! I'm here!"

"Who?" Edison asked.

"Qwerty Stevens!" Qwerty shouted.

"My God!" Edison exclaimed. He stopped, touching Qwerty's arm with his fingertips as if he needed proof the boy was real. "You figured out a way, didn't you?"

Qwerty nodded excitedly. Edison, who had seemed so ornery when Qwerty first saw him, softened instantly. A broad smile danced across his face. He wrapped his arm around Qwerty and led him outside the lab, where it was cooler and they could talk privately.

Main Street looked different from the Main Street Qwerty knew. Instead of cars, carriages were being pulled by horses. The Pizza Hut on the corner wasn't there. In its place was a tiny store that sold "dry goods," whatever those were. There was no Treats and Eats, Econo-Cleaners, or Fabulous Wall Coverings Factory Outlet. Where the strip mall had been, there was, incredibly, a farm.

But Qwerty barely noticed all the differences. He couldn't take his eyes off Edison.

"How does the machine work?" Qwerty hollered into Edison's ear. "How did you invent it?"

"A few years ago," Edison told the boy, "I was experimenting with acoustic telegraphy. Do you know what that is?"

"No."

"Doesn't matter," Edison continued. He beamed in on Qwerty with his eyes, as if to compensate for his difficulty in hearing. "One day I accidentally brushed a wire against the core of a vibrator magnet. The core of the magnet gave off bright sparks, even when they weren't conducting electric current. Those sparks didn't follow the laws of static electricity. I immediately seized upon this phenomenon. It represented the unconfined visual flight of energy through space. Are you following me?"

"I think so."

"The point is I had discovered a true unknown force, which I called etheric force. It was a radiant force somewhere between light and heat on one hand, and magnetism and electricity on the other. It was something new to science. Do you understand?"

"Not exactly," Qwerty admitted.

"Let me put it to you this way. There's a connection between all the natural governing forces of life—chemical, electrical, and magnetic. Knowing how these forces interact, I was able to build a machine that, I hoped, would be able to circumvent the limitations of space and time."

"The Anytime Anywhere Machine!" Qwerty marveled. "It works as a time machine, too."

"It must work, or you wouldn't be here," Edison proclaimed proudly as he lit the cigar he had been holding. "This is a glorious day for science."

A food vendor's wagon was parked along the street, and Edison offered to buy Qwerty anything he desired. He would have liked a good breakfast. But the man was selling all kinds of candy, and everything cost just a few pennies. Qwerty grabbed two cotton-candy packages, one to eat immediately and the other to save for later.

"Young man," Edison scolded, "you're digging your grave with your teeth."

"Aw, a little junk food never hurt anybody," Qwerty hollered.

"The human body is a machine," Edison said. "If you don't put the best fuel in that machine, it won't run properly."

"You sound like my mother."

"She sounds like a good woman," Edison said. "I'm sure she told you the secret to good health is mastication."

"I beg your pardon?" Qwerty asked.

"Chewing," Edison said. "Chew every piece of food until it's a liquid. That way you get every ounce of nourishment and energy from it."

Edison suddenly stopped walking and got down on his hands and knees. Qwerty joined him, peering at the ground. There was a row of anthills in the dirt. Edison stared intently at the colony of ants moving in and out of their holes.

"Look at them," he finally said. "There must be a million of them in there, living and working together. No fights. No problems. They all work toward a common goal. I don't care if it's 1879, 1979, or 2079, you'll never see human beings work together like that."

"I think you would like the future," Qwerty hollered at Edison. "We've got a lot of cool inventions. TVs, PCs, VCRs, DVDs—"

"Shhhh," Edison said, putting a finger to his lips. He got up, not bothering to brush the dirt off his pants. "Don't say another word about those things."

"Why not?"

"I don't want to know the inventions of the future," Edison said. "I want to invent them myself."

"If you don't want me to tell you about the future, why did you want me to come here?" Qwerty asked.

"Did you bring what I requested?" Edison asked anxiously, glancing at Qwerty's backpack.

"Your message broke up and I couldn't translate the end of it," Qwerty said. "Bring what?"

"An electric lamp!" Edison said sharply. "I called you here because I need a bulb."

"I'm sorry," Qwerty said sadly. "I didn't bring one."

Edison's shoulders slumped as he cursed to himself. He told Qwerty that he had been struggling for several years to invent an incandescent electric lamp. That is, a lamp that gave off a bright light when an electric current was passed through a substance he called a filament. The only problem was that he had not yet found a filament that would give off light without burning up.

"I tested coconut hair and fishing line," Edison said. "Hog bristles and porcupine quills. Spiderwebs. I tested every metal in existence. I tested six thousand different vegetable fibers. I tested everything from an elephant's hide to the eyebrows of a United States senator. Nothing works."

"And you thought that if somebody from the future brought you a bulb," Qwerty said, "you could crack it open and look inside?"

"Desperate times call for desperate measures," Edison sighed, hanging his head. "I have been sending out signals through my machine for months, hoping someone like you would receive them."

"You *will* invent the lightbulb," Qwerty assured Edison. "I mean, it says so in all the history books."

"That's gratifying, but it doesn't help me right now," Edison said. "I have a half dozen competitors trying to beat me to the solution. I'm running out of money for research. I already told the press that my lamp is finished, and promised them a demonstration by New Year's Eve. My reputation is at stake."

Edison gazed off into space for a moment, then he brightened and snapped his fingers.

"Wait a minute," he said to Qwerty. "You have electric lamps in your time, don't you?"

"Sure. In every room of the house."

"Then you *must* know what the filament is made from."

"Mr. Edison, I never looked inside a lightbulb. I didn't even know what a filament *was* until you just told me."

Edison slammed one fist against the other.

"I'm sorry," Qwerty said.

"It's not your fault," Edison said, turning back toward the lab. "It was a ridiculous idea anyway. I just have to keep searching. The answer is out there, waiting for me to discover it. It's teasing me, taunting me."

Edison shook his fist in the air and announced, "I will find you!"

"May I ask you a question?" Qwerty yelled at Edison. "Your machine—the one that brought me here—is an incredible invention. Why did you bury it in your backyard?"

"Bury it?" Edison said, surprised. "I didn't bury it."

"Then who did?"

CHAPTER 10

An Empty Bed

Barbara Stevens's alarm clock went off at six thirty, as it did every weekday morning. She was a drummer in the West Orange High School band, so she had to get up early for practice before school.

Half asleep, Barbara went to brush her teeth. On the way to the bathroom she noticed a piece of paper lying near her door. The paper said HIT ESCAPE KEY. But it was dark, and Barbara didn't notice the words. Absentmindedly she picked up the paper, crumpled it without reading it, and dropped it in her garbage can.

Quietly Barbara dressed, washed, and ate a quick

breakfast. When she left for school, she tiptoed across the living room so she wouldn't wake the rest of the family.

Madison woke up at seven thirty. She shuffled groggily out of bed and crawled into her mother's bed to cuddle. When the clock reached eight, Mrs. Stevens reluctantly pulled away from Madison's arms and went to turn on the shower to warm it up. By eight thirty she was dressed for work and Madison was ready to go to school. A neighbor who had a son in Madison's first-grade class stopped by and drove both kids to school.

Next it was time to get "Sleepyhead" up. Qwerty always slept later than everyone else. But after he woke up, he could brush his teeth, get dressed, and wolf down a bowl of cereal faster than anybody. Qwerty liked to stay up late playing with his computer, so Mrs. Stevens let him sleep as long as possible.

"Qwerty!" she called from downstairs. "Time to get up!"

When there was no answer, Mrs. Stevens went

upstairs and knocked softly on Qwerty's door.

"Breakfast is ready!" she said loudly enough to be heard, but quietly enough not to startle anyone out of a deep sleep.

Again, there was no response. Mrs. Stevens opened the door a crack. No Qwerty. The sheets and blankets were pulled back, so clearly the bed had been slept in. Mrs. Stevens ran her hand under the sheet, just to make sure Qwerty wasn't hiding in there. He wasn't.

Mrs. Stevens let out a scream and ran to the phone.

CHAPTER 11

The Boys in Room Number Five

Qwerty licked the last bits of cotton candy off his fingertips. Thomas Edison led him back to the laboratory. He no longer seemed upset that Qwerty hadn't brought a lightbulb with him. He was ready to get back to work.

"It's so hot in here," Edison said, holding the front door open for the boy, "I feel like taking off my flesh and sitting in my bones."

"You should invent air conditioning," Qwerty suggested. Edison didn't hear him. Even if he had, he wouldn't have known what Qwerty was talking about.

Qwerty followed Edison through a maze of work-shops buzzing with activity, until they reached a room that was separated from the rest of the laboratory. A large number five was on the door.

Edison ushered Qwerty inside. There was a group of men sitting around a large table. Some appeared to be young, a few of them barely twenty. It was hard to tell for sure, because all of them had a beard, a bushy mustache, or both. They were, for the most part, as slovenly as Edison.

"Boys," Edison announced, "I'd like to introduce you to my young friend, Qwerty Stevens. He's from—"

Qwerty was afraid Edison was going to finish his sentence with "the future." Instead, he winked at Qwerty and said, "He's from West Orange."

The men all grunted greetings. Edison introduced them one at a time, like a singer introducing his backup band.

"First we have John Ott, master draftsman," Edison said, pointing to the man at his left. "Then there's 'Honest John' Kruesi, machine maker extraordinaire. Next to Mr. Kruesi is Charles Batchelor, mechanical genius. Then we have Ludwig Boehm, an expert in the art of glassblowing. Francis Jehl is my personal assistant—"

"Personal slave, he means," Jehl joked.

"And last but not least is my man Culture."

"The name is Francis Upton," said the young man Edison called Culture. Unlike the others, he got up to shake Qwerty's hand. "I'm a specialist in mathematical physics. It is my pleasure to make your acquaintance."

"We keep Culture around in case we need to do any addin' or subtractin'," Edison cracked, spitting a piece of his cigar on the floor. "These are my top boys, my muckers. They muck around in dirt and filth and stench all day in search of the greater truths of the universe."

"And money," added John Ott.

"Edison is the chief mucker," Batchelor said, and everyone laughed heartily.

To Qwerty, Edison's inner circle looked more like a rowdy pirate crew than a group of scientists. And Edison was the captain of the ship.

Ludwig Boehm picked up a long tube and blew air through it until a shiny bubble of glass grew out of the other end. He turned the tube slowly with his fingers as he blew so the bulb would stay perfectly round. Then he detached the hot glass bulb with a metal tool and put the bulb in a pile with others he had completed.

Qwerty had replaced dozens of lightbulbs at home, but it never occurred to him that somebody or something had to mold the glass into the shape of a bulb.

In the corner of the room was a big iron machine with two upright columns about six feet high. The columns were wrapped with heavy wires. Somebody had put a makeshift sign on the machine that said LONG-WAISTED MARY ANN. Edison told Qwerty it was a dynamo that converted steam power into electrical energy. It would provide the current that would—hopefully—light up a bulb.

In another corner was a large machine that Edison called "Sprengel." It was a vacuum pump with a long handle sticking out of the side and a big glass dome on top. Edison explained that unless all the air was removed from the inside of a bulb, it would burn out almost instantly. Fire, Edison pointed out, can't exist in a vacuum.

The last piece of the puzzle, as Edison put it, was the filament—the thing inside the bulb that electric current would surge through. Edison and his team had been searching for a substance that could withstand tremendous heat and give off light without fusing or melting or burning out. So far, everything they tried had failed.

Edison pulled a wooden chair up to the table, where mountains of stuff had been piled. It looked like somebody had emptied a garbage can on the table.

"I'll pay a thousand dollars," Edison announced, "to the man who finds a filament that will glow for more than five minutes."

"Two thousand," suggested Charles Batchelor.

"You're on, Batch," agreed Edison.

Batchelor selected a piece of corn silk from the pile of junk on the table. He rubbed some gooey carbon paste over it and rolled it until the corn silk was black. Edison explained that carbon doesn't melt until it reaches 3,500 degrees Fahrenheit, so they carbonized every filament.

In fact, there was a shed in the back of the lab where kerosene lamps burned all day. At the end of the day the carbon was scraped off the lamps and made into this paste to carbonize lightbulb filaments.

There was a small brick oven near the door. Batchelor bent the corn silk filament into the shape of a horseshoe and baked it in the oven. Then he carefully inserted it into a bulb. He held it very delicately, as if he were holding a precious jewel.

John Kruesi placed the bulb inside the Sprengel, then pushed the handle of the pump up and down to suck the air from the bulb. Then the bulb was sealed and inserted into a socket.

"Light 'er up, Francis," ordered Edison.

Francis Jehl turned a dial on the dynamo to send electric current through the bulb. Everyone in the room stared at it.

The instant the current hit the corn silk, the bulb flared and blew out in a puff of smoke. Grunts, sighs, and curses were heard around the table.

"So much for corn silk," Francis Jehl said, carefully noting the date, time, and results of the experiment in a journal.

Batchelor removed the blown bulb and replaced it with a fresh one. He picked up a small piece of cedar bark from the table, carbonized it, and sealed it in the bulb. When the electric current went through the cedar bark, it melted without giving any light at all. Francis Jehl dutifully wrote down the negative result in the journal.

As the day wore on, Edison and his men tried filaments they made from chromium, nickel, old carpets, flax, hickory, twine, walrus hides, turnips, pumpkins, squash, eggplants, hemp, horsehair, shark teeth, deer horns, turtle shells, cork, rubber, even Limburger cheese and macaroni. None of them glowed for more than a second or two.

The filaments melted and sparked. Sometimes the bulb would explode, and everybody would duck their head as bits of glass flew around the room.

After an unsuccessful test of a carbonized grasshopper leg, there was a knock at the door. Edison let a man in and embraced him warmly.

"Smitty, you're back!" Edison said excitedly. "Did you get it?"

Wordlessly the man called Smitty handed Edison a round piece of wood that looked like bamboo. As Edison broke off a thin piece and carbonized it, he explained to Qwerty that he had sent Smitty all the way to India in search of this specific type of wood he thought could work as a filament.

Edison personally inserted the new filament into a bulb, pumped out the air, sealed it, and sent an electric current through it.

The bulb glowed, then burned out in less than two seconds.

"Try China," Edison said, patting Smitty on the shoulder and showing him the door.

"It's useless," John Ott moaned. It was around four o'clock in the afternoon by that time.

Edison paced around the room, his hands thrust in his pockets. He stared at the floor, his hair falling over his face. He looked like a man possessed. Instead of being disappointed by the failures, he appeared to be motivated by them. He seemed to have supreme confidence that if he tried enough different substances, eventually he would find the one that worked.

"No experiments are useless," he insisted. "Negative results are just what I want. They're just as valuable to me as positive results. With every failure I learn another thing that doesn't work."

The rest of the team, however, was getting discouraged, and Edison knew it. He called for some food to be brought in, clearing all the junk off the table so the men would have room to eat. Francis Upton, the man Edison called Culture, cranked up a phonograph, and the tinny sound of Beethoven's Ninth Symphony filled the room.

"The boys need a little inspiration to keep up their morale," Edison whispered to Qwerty. "Got any ideas?"

"I could tell them I come from the future," Qwerty whispered, "and that my house has lightbulbs in every room."

"They'll think you're a lunatic," Edison said. He took some turkey from a platter and pulled a chair up to the table.

"One day when I was a little boy," Edison told the group, "I saw a bird eat a worm and then fly away."

The men turned their attention to Edison. He loved telling stories, and they loved listening to them.

"I came to the conclusion, naturally enough, that birds must be able to fly *because* they eat worms," Edison continued. Some of the men smiled.

"So I did a little experiment to test my theory. I got a dozen worms and mashed them up. Then, when my mother wasn't looking, I put them into the bowl of mashed potatoes she was going to be serving for dinner that night. I figured that if my theory was correct, the whole family would be able to fly."

"What happened?" Qwerty asked.

"The theory was wrong," Edison laughed. "Nobody flew. But when I told them what I'd done, they *did* fly out of the house to go vomit in the yard!"

The muckers thought that was the funniest thing they had ever heard, and Edison was pleased to have improved their spirits a little.

"So, boys," Edison reminded them, "even when we fail, we learn something. We learn what *doesn't* work. We may have to test every single substance on this planet. Because *one* of them is going make this son of a—" Edison looked at Qwerty before continuing. "*One* of them is going to make this thing glow like the sun."

As the muckers ate their dinner Edison told them of the new and fantastic inventions he was planning to create after the electric light was perfected. He would invent a flying machine, he insisted. He described a future device that would transmit pictures over telephone lines. He dreamed of building a machine that could hypnotize people. He would create moving pictures and project them on a screen for people to view. He imagined a day when people would live in concrete houses, with concrete furniture, even concrete pianos.

Qwerty listened, with rapt attention. Some of Edison's predictions would come true, while others would be failures. And only *he* knew which was which.

CHAPTER 12

Missing Persons

When she didn't find him sleeping in his bed that morning, Qwerty's mother got on the phone with the police immediately. A patrol car pulled up four minutes later. Two officers got out of the car to find Mrs. Stevens sitting on her front porch sobbing.

"He ran away," she cried. "I know he ran away."

"Mrs. Stevens," one of the officers said gently. "What makes you think your son ran away?"

"I scolded him several times in the last few days for going out without my permission. He did it again, so I grounded him for a week. The other day he threatened to go away forever, and I guess he did. It's all my fault."

Mrs. Stevens broke down, unable to continue. One of the officers went to the patrol car while the other tried to comfort her. He gave Mrs. Stevens the speech he had delivered to all too many parents during his years on the police force.

"You did the best thing by calling in a missing-person report so quickly," the officer explained. "Right now we can't consider this a runaway child, a kidnapping, or even a crime. We just don't have all the facts. My partner is issuing a BOLO bulletin right now. That means 'be on the lookout.' Are you with me, Mrs. Stevens?"

"Yes," she sniffled.

"I need you to do exactly what I say. This is important. Do not touch or remove anything from your son's room. Don't clean his room or wash his clothes. You may be contaminating evidence. Even a garbage can may contain clues that will help lead to the recovery of your son.

"Don't touch anything that might have your son's

fingerprints, DNA, or scent on it. That includes hair-brushes, bedsheets, or even a pencil with bite marks. With a good set of fingerprints or DNA we may be able to tell if your son has been in a particular car or house.

"Be prepared to answer a lot of hard, repetitive questions by investigators. We know this is difficult, Mrs. Stevens, but when a child is missing, anyone who knows that child has to be considered a suspect. A large number of children are harmed by a member of their own family. You should expect to be asked to take a polygraph test. That's standard procedure."

"I understand."

"If you want to hire a private detective, that's up to you. But we advise against hiring psychics or other people who claim to be able to find missing persons. We also do not recommend your offering a cash reward for your son's return. It can lead to a lot of problems. And if anyone contacts you asking for money in exchange for the return of your son, report it to us immediately.

"Above all, Mrs. Stevens, we need you to be physically and mentally strong and attend to your own needs as the search goes on. It may be hard right now for you to maintain your daily routine, but you must. Force yourself to eat and sleep. Your life must go on. You should get in touch with friends, acquaintances, extended-family members, or anyone who might have seen your son before he disappeared. And we need you to be here in case your son calls or returns home."

"But I want to help in the search," protested Mrs. Stevens.

"The best thing you can do is provide information to investigators. We'll be bringing in tracking dogs. If your son is anywhere in the area, they'll find him. They'll be putting a tap on your phone too. That's also standard procedure.

"And Mrs. Stevens, don't blame yourself for what happened. It's not your fault that your son isn't home with you right now. We're going to do all we can to bring him home safely."

When school was over, Barbara Stevens went straight to her Poetry Club meeting. Then she gathered up her books and hurried home. She remembered that she was grounded, and today was the day she and Qwerty were going to use the Anytime Anywhere Machine to send him on a trip.

By the time Barbara got home, bloodhounds were running around the house, and investigators were going door-to-door questioning neighbors.

"What's going on?" Barbara asked Madison, who was sitting on the sidewalk and drawing with colored chalk.

"Qwerty is missing!" Madison sobbed, wrapping her arms around her sister and hugging her tightly. "Mom thinks he ran away from home."

Ran away from home? Barbara knew Qwerty. He would never run away. But he might have—

There was a policeman standing at the front of the house. Barbara went around the back and opened the door. She dashed up the stairs, threw her schoolbooks on her bed, and rushed into Qwerty's room.

The computer was on and Qwerty's photo was in the scanner. Barbara always told Qwerty he should turn the computer *off* every night, but Qwerty always insisted it used less power to leave it on all the time.

Barbara clicked off the screen saver. The Edison Web site filled the screen.

"Silly boy," clucked Barbara. "He just sent himself to the Edison Laboratory down the road!"

Barbara was right. Qwerty was at the Edison Laboratory. What she didn't know was that Qwerty was at the Edison Laboratory *in 1879*.

Barbara figured she could bring Qwerty back with a tap of the ESCAPE key. But what fun would that be? Instead, she decided to surprise him. She picked up the photo of herself that she had used to go to Treats and Eats and slipped it into the scanner. She scanned herself and hit the ENTER key.

Like that, she vanished.

"Madison," Mrs. Stevens asked her daughter. "Is Barbara home yet?"

"I saw her go around the back, Mommy," Madison replied.

"When?"

"A few minutes ago."

Mrs. Stevens walked around the back of the house but didn't see Barbara. She went inside to look for her. Barbara wasn't downstairs watching TV or in the kitchen raiding the refrigerator. She wasn't in her room doing her homework, though her schoolbooks were on her bed.

"Barbara!" Mrs. Stevens hollered. There was no answer. She walked briskly around the house, a sense of urgency in her step, shouting Barb's name. Nobody answered.

Mrs. Stevens broke down.

"Now my *daughter* is missing!" she screamed.

CHAPTER 13

A Little Star

The sun set over the Edison Laboratory on October 21, 1879.

In room 5 Edison's inner circle were finishing their dinner. Qwerty Stevens went to use the bathroom. While he was out of the room, the strangest thing happened.

Barbara Stevens suddenly appeared, out of nowhere, standing in the middle of the table.

The first reaction from the men in room 5 was shocked disbelief. It wasn't every day that a sixteen-year-old girl suddenly appeared out of nowhere, without any warning. Edison was called a wizard, but he wasn't known for performing magic tricks.

After staring at Barbara for a moment, John Ott put his fingers in his mouth and let out a loud wolf whistle. The other men, with the exception of Francis Upton, began to clap their hands with approval and stomp their feet on the wood floor. Edison beamed with delight.

Barbara looked around at the men, disgusted, and put her hands on her hips. "Shut up!" she shouted. "You're a bunch of sexist pigs!"

When Qwerty returned from the bathroom, there was stunned silence in room 5.

"Barb!" Qwerty yelled. She jumped off the table and hugged him.

"I knew you wouldn't run away," Barbara whispered to him. "I'll never call you Nerdy again."

"And I'll never call you Thing One again."

"Is she your lady?" Francis Upton inquired of Qwerty.

"She's my sister," Qwerty replied.

"Where are we?" Barbara asked. "I was only

trying to send myself down the street to the Edison Laboratory."

"You *did*," Qwerty informed her. "But you sent yourself to 1879."

"I didn't know the machine could send us through *time*."

"Neither did I."

Edison and his men watched Barbara with fascination. "What's the gal talking about?" Batchelor asked.

"Must be a loony," Kruesi replied. "Look how she's dressed. She ought to be in an asylum."

"Qwerty," Barbara whispered, "who *are* these jerks?"

"They're not jerks. They're brilliant men of science. And this," Qwerty said as he led her to Edison, "is their boss."

"Pleased to meet you, miss," Edison said politely. "I'm Tom Edison."

Barbara looked at the great inventor with wonder in her eyes. Then those eyes rolled back in her head and she went limp. Qwerty caught her as she slumped to the floor.

"The ladies just adore me, don't they, fellows?" Edison told the men, who erupted into laughter.

Francis Upton, who had some training in medicine, wet a cloth and rushed to Barbara's side. He was able to revive her and cradled her in his arms gently.

"Allow me to apologize for the behavior of my associates," Upton explained when Barbara opened her eyes. "These gentlemen haven't seen a lady in weeks."

"And most of us are *married*!" Edison cracked, prompting the others to laugh uproariously again.

"Shut your mugs, you Neanderthals," Upton scolded the others before turning his attention back to Barbara. "They certainly have never seen a young lady so lovely as yourself."

"Listen to Culture," Edison snorted. "If only he could find me a filament as well as he can woo a lady."

Once Barbara had fully recovered, she got up and grabbed Qwerty. "Everyone thinks you ran away," she said urgently. "They've got the police looking for you and everything. We gotta get back."

"Okay," Qwerty agreed. "But first I want to see this."

The men began to clear their plates off the table and put back the electrical equipment they had been experimenting with.

"What are they doing?" Barbara asked.

"Trying to invent the electric light," Qwerty whispered.

"You didn't happen to bring a bulb along, did you?" Edison asked Barbara.

It was getting dark outside. The other workers at the Edison Lab had gone home for the day. But Batchelor, Kruesi, Upton, Boehm, and Ott called themselves the Insomnia Squad. They were Edison's most trusted and loyal men, perfectly happy to work all night if necessary. And with Edison, it was often necessary.

As daylight disappeared the Insomnia Squad lit matches and turned on gaslights and kerosene lamps so they could see what they were doing. Even so, room 5 grew dim. The light flickered with every breeze, and the unpleasant smell of burning kerosene filled the room. Qwerty and Barbara felt uncomfortable with an open flame burning so close by.

It was difficult for them to understand that the whole world used to be like that every day after the sun went down. For the first time they appreciated the soft, warm glow of incandescent light.

The presence of a female in the room seemed to give Edison's "boys" a boost of new enthusiasm. It almost seemed as though they were showing off for Barbara, like a bunch of schoolboys trying to impress the girls on the playground at recess.

After the bulb apparatus had been set up again, Batchelor took off his shoe and put the shoelace inside a bulb to see if it would glow. Edison went one better. He had carefully removed the skin off the top of his pudding from dinner and somehow managed to carbonize it. Both experiments were dismal failures, as Francis Jehl noted in his ever present journal.

"Give me a hunk of your beard," Kruesi commanded Francis Upton, grabbing at Upton's chin.

"I will not!" Upton replied indignantly.

"Come on," Kruesi insisted. "Your whiskers may be the perfect filament!"

"Get your filthy hands off me, you barbarian!" Upton shouted.

"Do it for science!" yelled Batchelor, who jumped on Upton. With the help of Ott and Kruesi, they wrestled him to the ground.

"Boys will be boys." Edison smirked, spitting out a chunk of his cigar.

"That's disgusting," Barbara said, apparently no longer in awe of the great inventor. "Don't you use a spittoon or something?"

"It's so hard to hit a spittoon," Edison commented, "and it's almost impossible to miss the floor."

After they had succeeded in removing a piece of Francis Upton's beard, Batchelor carbonized it and carefully inserted it into a glass bulb. Rubbing his chin, Francis Upton apologized to Barbara once again for the immature behavior of his colleagues. With a bow, he told her that a young woman as lovely as herself should not be subjected to the obnoxious behavior of "subhumans."

"Douse the lights," Edison ordered once the beard bulb was ready. "Turn on the juice, slowly."

Out of the darkness a cherry red glow appeared from the bulb. It didn't flicker, and it didn't flare. All eyes in the room stared intently at the tiny light.

"A little more juice," Edison whispered when the light had burned for five seconds. The bulb glowed brighter, like a little star.

"Ten amperes of current," Francis Upton said, peering at some dials before him. "Ten volts. Resistance is two hundred seventy-five ohms. Twenty candlepower."

"A little more," Edison said. The bulb had been burning for fifteen seconds.

The added current was too much for the little strand of hair. It burned brightly for another second, lighting up the room. Then there was the sound of a single *pop*, and the light went out, plunging room 5 into darkness.

"We're getting close," Edison said as he lit a gaslight. "Very close."

"I bet Upton's armpit hair would do the trick!"

Kruesi suggested cheerfully. Before they could grab him, the normally reserved Francis Upton slugged John Kruesi in the jaw.

While the Insomnia Squad were deciding what substance to test next, Qwerty pulled out the package of cotton candy Edison had bought him earlier in the day.

"Gimme a chunk of that," Edison said, pinching off a piece. Batchelor, always at the ready, carbonized a thin strand of the candy and bent it into a horseshoe shape. Edison inserted it into a fresh bulb. Kruesi exhausted the bulb of air and sealed it.

"Light 'er up, Mr. Jehl!" Edison commanded.

Current surged through the cotton candy. It glowed for an instant. Then the bulb exploded. Glass flew all over the room, and everyone hid their face.

"Cotton candy!" Edison snickered as the mess was cleaned up. "What a silly idea." He noticed Qwerty picking shards of glass out of his T-shirt and asked the boy if he had been hurt.

"I'm fine," Qwerty replied.

"Wait a minute!" Edison suddenly said. "Your shirt! Cotton! Have we tried cotton?"

"No," Francis Jehl reported, paging through his journal. "Wool, yes. Burlap, yes. Many other fibers. But never cotton."

"Take your shirt off," Edison commanded Qwerty.

"Why?"

"Just take it off. I want to try something."

Qwerty pulled his T-shirt over his head. Edison cut a small piece from the shirt with scissors and teased out a thread of cotton fiber. He carbonized it himself and prepared a new bulb.

"Light 'er up, Mr. Jehl!" Edison commanded.

The little cotton filament took the electric current and held it. A faint but steady light could be seen. Edison requested more juice, and the bulb glowed brighter. He asked for still more, and the whole room was bathed in a warm, white light. It was now brighter in room 5 than it had been with the gaslight.

Everyone gasped, including Qwerty and Barbara,

who had seen *millions* of lightbulbs in their time and never given them a second thought.

"Full power," Edison demanded after the bulb had glowed for a minute.

With heat surging through it that would melt a diamond, the fragile piece of cotton glowed even *more* brightly. The light was so bright it was impossible to look at it without squinting. It wasn't going out!

The Insomnia Squad began to cheer, jump up and down, hug each other, and whoop with the pure joy of working so long and so hard to create something so wonderful. Nobody bothered turning on the gaslights. They weren't necessary. The little bulb lit up the whole room.

"Gentlemen," Edison announced when the bulb had burned steadily for five minutes, "welcome to the age of electric light."

"Does this mean the kid gets the two thousand dollars?" Batchelor asked Edison. But the great inventor was transfixed, staring into the bulb with wonder.

T. A. EDISON.
Electric-Lamp.

No. 223,898.   Patented Jan. 27, 1880.

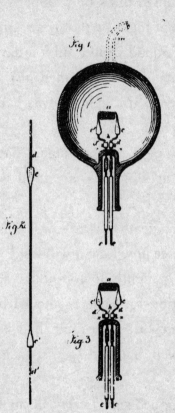

"Cotton!" he said, almost in a daze. "Probably the most abundant fiber on the planet! Cheap and easy to grow. Why didn't I think of it sooner?"

It was late at night by that time. One would think the Insomnia Squad would call it a day, tired and triumphant. They didn't. The men just sat and stared silently at the electric light. It was hard for them to believe it was real.

"Don't you guys ever go home?" Barbara asked.

"Nothin' at home is as good as this," said Batchelor.

"We're on a death watch now," Edison explained. "We want to see how long it will last."

Staring at a lightbulb for hours didn't hold the same fascination for Qwerty and Barbara, however. Twenty minutes after the bulb had begun to glow, they were asleep, huddled against each other in their chairs.

Edison scooped up Qwerty in his arms. Francis Upton lovingly picked up Barbara like she was an injured bird. They carried the sleeping children into Edison's private library, where he kept a cot for those rare occasions when he would submit to sleep himself.

But there would be little sleep for Thomas Edison tonight.

CHAPTER 14
Questions and Answers

When it was discovered that *two* of the Stevens children had disappeared, every police officer in West Orange was put on the case. The investigative team in charge of missing persons were not just puzzled, they were humiliated. Barbara Stevens had disappeared right under their noses. Police protection was provided for six-year-old Madison, to be certain nothing happened to her. A team of forensic scientists from Washington was being assembled to come to New Jersey and scour Qwerty's room for clues.

In the meantime, reporters swarmed to the

Stevenses' house, trying to get interviews with Mrs. Stevens. But she wasn't talking. She was in a state of shock. All she could do was sit in her kitchen, thinking of what she might have done or said to drive Qwerty and Barbara away.

The police, however, were no longer filing the Stevenses' case under "RUNAWAY CHILDREN." With the disappearance of Barbara they decided that kidnapping was more likely. The first suspect they brought in for questioning was Qwerty's friend Joey Dvorak.

Joey was nervous and fidgety when the West Orange police asked if he would come in for what they called a "little chat." Joey's father was a lawyer, and he advised his son to answer the questions simply and honestly, but not to say a single word more than was necessary. Mr. Dvorak sat at his son's side while the police questioned him.

"Qwerty is your best friend, isn't he, Joey?" the investigator asked.

"Yes."

"Anything you want to tell us, Joey? Anything you want to get off your chest?"

"No."

"Do you know where Qwerty and his sister Barbara are?"

"No."

"What do you think happened to Qwerty and Barbara?"

"I don't know."

"Care to take a guess?"

"You don't have to answer that, Joey," Mr. Dvorak interrupted.

"I don't have a guess," Joey replied.

"Did you and Qwerty have an argument recently?" the investigator continued.

"No."

"Joey, did you do anything to Qwerty and Barbara Stevens?"

"No."

"Are you telling us the truth?"

"Yes."

It went on like that for a while. The investigator didn't jump to the conclusion that Joey was lying just because he was nervous and fidgety during his interview. Lots of thirteen-year-old kids would be frightened in a situation like that. But the cops weren't convinced that Joey was innocent, either.

The morning after Qwerty and Barbara disappeared, the story had already hit the local TV news and newspapers.

WEST ORANGE TEENS VANISH

WEST ORANGE—A 13-year-old boy and his 16-year-old sister disappeared from their Llewellyn Park home yesterday, police announced today. Investigators are searching the area for Barbara Stevens and Robert Edward Stevens, who is known as "Qwerty."

The odd thing about this case is that the two teens vanished separately. First, Qwerty was not in his bed on the morning of October 21. Later in the day, even as the police were investigating the boy's disappearance, his sister came home from school and then vanished without a trace.

Investigators appear to be treating the case as a kidnapping. A close friend of Qwerty Stevens's has been questioned. Police would not reveal the boy's name because he is a minor.

"All I want is my children back," said an anguished Dana Stevens, the mother of the missing teens.

Qwerty Stevens is a short, serious boy with short, dark hair who loves basketball. Barbara Stevens is a tall, slim girl with long, dark hair who plays drums and enjoys poetry. Anyone with information should contact the West Orange Police Department immediately.

Thousands of people in the New Jersey and New York area read that article. One of them was Ashley Quadrel, the man who had been poking around West

Orange asking questions about Thomas Edison the night before Qwerty disappeared.

Quadrel was sipping coffee and reading his morning paper at the offices of the Sixth Sense Institute, a company that studied paranormal phenomenon.

It just doesn't make sense, Quadrel thought. *Two kids in the same family don't just disappear one after the other.*

He remembered talking to that Stevens kid who lived next door to Edison's house. He remembered that during their brief conversation Qwerty had stepped on his sister's foot, as if he didn't want her to say something. He remembered the hole in the backyard of their house.

Ashley Quadrel put down his coffee mug and smiled.

They found it! Those kids found the Anytime Anywhere Machine. They must have used it to send themselves someplace. That's why nobody can find those kids!

The Stevens kids could be anyplace—possibly in any time period, it suddenly occurred to Quadrel.

Unless there was a way to reverse the process, they might never be heard from again. It would be like they had vanished off the face of the earth.

Quadrel's mind was racing now. He went into the storage room across the hall from his office. He looked around to see if anyone was watching him. He closed the door behind him.

There was a safe in the storage room that contained important documents and some money. Only a few people in the company knew the combination to the safe, and Quadrel was one of them.

He opened the safe and removed ten thousand dollars.

CHAPTER 15
An Hour or a Lifetime

"Rise and shine!" Edison said cheerfully, not more than five hours after Qwerty and Barbara had dozed off. "The light still burns!"

"Did you sleep at all?" Qwerty asked groggily.

"I took a quick catnap on the floor," Edison replied.

"Don't you need more sleep than that?" asked Barbara.

"Fish don't sleep!" Edison said. "Why should people? I can't get anything done while I'm sleeping. It's a waste of precious time. The electric light will reduce human dependency on this barbaric custom."

"I'm tired," Qwerty moaned, rolling over in the cot.

When Barbara got up, she found an envelope that someone must have placed next to her while she was sleeping. She opened it.

Miss Stevens,

May I request the very great pleasure of escorting you to tea at any time that may suit your convenience? To grant this favor will give me very much pleasure. No pains will be spared by myself to have you enjoy the occasion, and I will consult your wishes in every particular as to time of calling for you and returning.

Waiting an early reply to this, I remain,

Most sincerely,

Francis Upton

"Who's Francis Upton?" Barbara asked.

"My mathematician," Edison replied. "The gentleman whose beard we tested in a bulb last night. I believe he's sweet on you."

Barbara laughed and tossed the note aside.

Edison was in a jolly mood as he wheeled in breakfast on a cart. The lightbulb with a cotton filament had been glowing for almost six hours, he explained, and it was showing no signs of burnout. He was hoping for ten, or maybe twenty, hours if he was lucky.

"Mutton?" Edison asked.

"No, thanks," Barbara replied. "I never eat dead sheep this early in the morning. We should really be getting home."

Qwerty and Barbara's house was only a half a mile from the Edison Laboratory. It would be simple to walk home. There was only one problem: Nobody would be there for more than a hundred years.

In the excitement over the electric light it hadn't occurred to either Qwerty or Barbara how they would get back to the twenty-first century. They couldn't just walk home, because their house wouldn't be built for sixty years. They couldn't call their mother on the phone. Although the telephone did exist, *she* did not.

"I have an idea," Edison said.

He led Qwerty and Barbara to a small, private office behind the library. Edison called it his "secret hiding place" because only a few of his closest associates knew about it. The room was nearly bare, except for a telegraph key that was hooked up to a small machine. Upon close inspection Qwerty could see that the machine was identical to the Anytime Anywhere Machine he had dug up in his backyard.

"If you were able to use this machine to send yourselves here," Edison reasoned, "you should be able to use it to send yourselves back."

"But back home the machine is hooked up to a computer," Qwerty told Edison. "That's how it sent us here."

"A what?"

"A personal computer," Qwerty explained. "It's a machine that can be used to write letters, draw pictures, send information over telephone lines—"

"What a marvelous device!" exclaimed Edison. "Who was the inventor of that?"

"I don't know," Qwerty replied. "But I think your

machine is useless without a computer."

"Not entirely useless," Edison said. "I used it to contact you. We can use it to contact someone else."

"•— •••• ——— —•— —," he tapped on the telegraph key. "•— •••• ——— —•— —."

There was no response. Nobody was sitting at Qwerty's computer to hit the ESCAPE key. The police had specifically asked that Qwerty's room not be disturbed.

Qwerty was getting frustrated. "If *you* had stayed home," he snapped at Barbara, "you would *be* there right now to get this message and bring me back."

"If *you* hadn't left without telling me, I *would* have been there to bring you back," Barbara protested.

"Didn't you get my note?"

"What note?"

"The note I left under your bedroom door."

Barbara gulped. "I didn't see it. And anyway, how was I supposed to know the thing would send me to 1879? I thought I was just going up the street."

"Now we're stuck here," Qwerty said bitterly. "Forever!"

At that, Qwerty and Barbara began to cry.

"So you're giving up, is that it?" Edison interrupted. "You tried one little thing and it didn't work, so you're giving up?"

Qwerty and Barbara wiped their tears and looked at Edison.

"Failure should push you forward, not back," Edison continued. "I could have given up on the electric light after the first filament blew out. After the first five *thousand* filaments blew out. But I didn't. People say I'm a genius. Well, genius is one percent inspiration and ninety-nine percent perspiration. I *never* quit until I get what I want. And I'm not going to quit until I figure out a way to get you two home."

Qwerty and Barbara felt ashamed for giving up so easily. With the greatest inventor in history working on their problem, they agreed, they were sure to be home in a matter of hours. Until then, they accepted Edison's offer to become "honorary muckers" for the day.

News of the electric light had spread through the laboratory that morning. As Edison led Qwerty and

Barbara around, workers came over to congratulate him on his latest success.

"We can build anything from a lady's watch to a locomotive in here," Edison boasted as he led Qwerty to the machine shop. "I'm going to start you out as a bottle monkey."

A bottle monkey was a boy who cleaned out glass test tubes, beakers, jars, glasses, and bottles that were used in the lab, especially in chemistry experiments. It wasn't hard work, but Qwerty had to wear thick gloves to prevent dangerous chemicals from touching his skin.

Every half hour Qwerty would take a break and go to Edison's secret hiding place to tap at the telegraph key:

But there was never anyone in Qwerty's room to receive the message.

While Qwerty labored in the machine shop, Edison led Barbara to another building on the complex.

"You'll be working with one of my favorite inventions," Edison said as he ushered her inside.

Dozens of women were stationed at tables around the room. On each table was a bunch of dolls. They were about two feet high and made of tin. Their dainty arms and legs moved. The dolls were outfitted with long brown hair, a turquoise silk dress, a hat, and little shoes. They had a bunch of tiny holes in their stomach, which looked like the nozzle of a showerhead.

Otherwise, they looked like ordinary dolls. But when Barbara got closer, she could see that the workers were inserting a tiny phonograph into the back of each doll.

"See?" Edison said as he picked one up. "They talk."

He turned a knob on the back of the doll and a disembodied voice crackled, "'Mary had a little lamb, / Its fleece was white as snow, / And everywhere that Mary went, / The lamb was sure to go.'"

"Cool," Barbara said, "but why is it all women in here?"

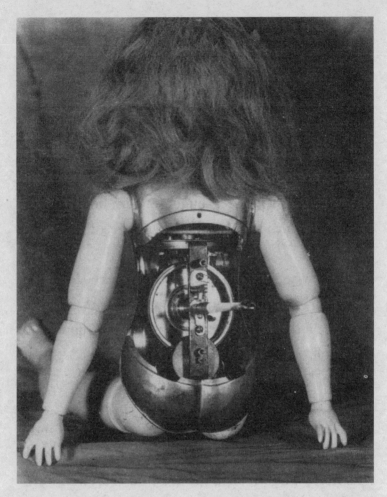

"A woman's fingers are more nimble," Edison
explained. "Your work is always neat. Women can do
many things better than men. That's how we are able

to crank out five hundred of these a day."

"That's a pretty sexist attitude," Barbara snorted. But the great inventor didn't hear her and was already on to the next task of his busy day.

The girl at the table behind Barbara showed her how to assemble the dolls. First, it was necessary to recite the nursery rhyme into the little phonograph. Then the phonograph was carefully inserted into the doll's back and sealed up with tiny screws.

After putting together about twenty dolls in two hours, Barbara was exhausted. Her back was sore from leaning over, and her eyes were bloodshot from working with the little parts. She swore that if she ever had children, she would let them play all the video games they wanted, as long as they never asked for a doll.

Fortunately, just before lunchtime, a visitor arrived and asked to see Barbara.

"Miss Stevens," the bearded man said with a graceful bow. "It is a joy to see your lovely face once again. Your complexion is clear as the conscience of a baby angel."

"Oh, hi, Mister . . . uh . . ."

"Upton," the man replied, handing Barbara a bouquet of flowers. "Francis Upton. We met last evening. The experience, for me, was as incandescent as the bulb that shone so brightly and continues to shine today, along with my thoughts of you."

"It's nice to see you again too, Mr. Upton." Barbara blushed.

"Miss Stevens, I hope I would not be too forward by asking if I may have the pleasure of sitting with you this evening?"

"Well, I expect to be gone by tonight," Barbara said.

"But if you are not?" Upton asked hopefully. "Might I sit with you then?"

"Okay, I guess."

"My heart is aflutter!" Upton bubbled, bowing again as he backed away.

The girl at the table next to Barbara's came over, all excited and giggly.

"He's very handsome!" she whispered to Barbara.

"He's kinda hot, I guess."

"Are you going to marry him?"

"Marry him?!" Barbara laughed. "I'm only six-teen!"

"Dearie, lots of girls are married by the time they're sixteen."

Being a bottle monkey was tiring, but Qwerty kept at it all day. Every half hour he would faithfully go to Edison's secret room and try to send a message home. Each time there was no response. There was nobody at the computer to receive the message.

At the end of the day Qwerty and Barbara reported to Edison's office. They were anxious to see if the great inventor had figured out a way to get them home.

"Almost fourteen hours the light burned!" Edison reported gleefully when he saw them. "We've already fired up another one! How are my new muckers?"

"If I have to recite 'Mary Had a Little Lamb' one more time, I think I'll shoot myself," Barbara said, making Edison chuckle.

"I'm wiped," Qwerty said, flopping into Edison's

chair. "Didn't you ever hear of child labor laws?"

"No," Edison replied honestly as he reached into his pocket. "Let's see, you both worked for ten hours today. At ten cents an hour, Qwerty earned one dollar."

He pulled off a bill and handed it to Qwerty. It didn't look exactly like a modern bill. George Washington was on the front, but so was Christopher Columbus.

"You're only paying him one lousy dollar for a whole day's work? That's *it*?"

"Plus seventy-five cents for you," Edison said, handing Barbara some coins.

"How come Qwerty got a dollar, and I get only seventy-five cents?"

"Because he worked in the machine shop," Edison explained.

"Why couldn't I work in the machine shop?" Barbara asked.

"I don't allow girls in the machine shop. It's too dangerous."

"That's not fair!" Barbara complained.

"Take my stupid dollar," Qwerty told Barbara. "I just want to go home. Have you figured out a way to get us out of here yet?"

"I'm working on it," Edison said.

"Well, how long is it going to take?"

"It could be an hour," Edison replied, "or it could be a lifetime. I have no idea. It usually takes me from five to seven years to perfect anything."

"Years?!"

CHAPTER 16

An Uninvited Guest

The West Orange Police Department stationed a patrol car outside the Stevenses' home all day. With two children missing, the WOPD wasn't taking any chances. They weren't going to let anything happen to Madison.

But at five o'clock that afternoon, during the two minutes when the police were changing shifts, Ashley Quadrel made his move.

He had come on foot. Ducking through alleys, he made it to the side of the Stevenses' house without being seen.

Quadrel knew the house well. Earlier in the day, as reporters gathered outside, Quadrel had checked the place out. The drainpipe next to a second-floor bedroom window, he had noticed, could be climbed. The basketball stickers on the window suggested it was Qwerty's bedroom.

With one patrol car gone for the day, and the next one yet to arrive, Quadrel shimmied up the drainpipe. He wore a backpack containing the ten thousand dollars he had removed from the safe in his office. He had also come prepared with a glass-cutting tool, but he didn't need it. Reaching over from the drainpipe at the second floor, he simply lifted Qwerty's window up and climbed in.

Qwerty's room, under strict orders from the police, had been photographed and the door locked after Barbara disappeared. It was obvious that the forensic team had not yet come to search for clues. The room was a mess, and Quadrel had to be careful not to step on Qwerty's wires, cables, audio-video gear, and other junk. Moving silently, like a good burglar, Quadrel tiptoed to the computer. Following the cables out the back of it, he found the Anytime Anywhere Machine on the floor, hidden among Qwerty's junk.

He stopped to marvel at it for a moment, then went back to the computer. Lifting the lid on the scanner, Quadrel found the photos of Qwerty and Barbara. *Those kids sent themselves somewhere,* he thought. *But where?*

He clicked the mouse to get rid of the screen saver. The Edison National Historic Site's Web page was on the screen. The time line was set at 1879. *Perfect,* Quadrel thought, as he fiddled with the computer.

He took his wallet out of his pocket and searched for something with his photo on it. The picture on his driver's license wasn't very flattering, but it would do.

Meanwhile, in Edison's laboratory, Qwerty decided to try just one more "ahoy" before calling it quits for the day. He went to the telegraph key and tapped the message out wearily.

Seconds later the key started tapping back.

"There's somebody there!" Qwerty hollered.

"They can bring us back home!"

"Who is it?" Barbara asked. "Mom?"

The dots and dashes came too fast for Qwerty to understand. But Edison was skilled in Morse code and read the message perfectly.

"SO . . . YOU . . . AREN'T . . . MISSING . . . AFTER . . . ALL," he repeated as the dots and dashes came in. "YOU'RE . . . TAKING . . . A . . . LITTLE TRIP . . . AREN'T . . . YOU?"

"Tell 'em to hit the ESCAPE key!" Qwerty yelled frantically.

But Ashley Quadrel had no intention of hitting the ESCAPE key. He had no interest in bringing the Stevens children back to their home. What he intended, rather, was to send *himself* to 1879. He scanned his driver's license into the computer and hit the ENTER key.

Instantly, he was standing in the same room with Qwerty, Barbara, and Edison.

"It works!" Quadrel exclaimed.

"Who are *you*?" Edison asked, shocked to see a

strange man in his secret room. "How did you get in here?"

"You're the guy who came to our house the other day," Barbara said. "You were asking questions about Mr. Edison."

"That's right," Quadrel replied. "Mr. Edison, my name is Ashley Quadrel, and I am very honored to meet you—"

"Is this man a friend of yours?" interrupted Edison.

"No," said Qwerty.

"I'm going to call the cops."

"Please don't do that, sir," Quadrel begged. "I'm a bit of an inventor myself. I lived through the 1970s, the 1980s, and the 1990s. I know about every major invention of the last century. I can show you how to make the first radio, the first television, years before their time. I'll help you build the first camcorder, the first personal computer. Let's go into business together. As a team, we can make millions. We can build the future."

"I'll build the future on my own," Edison said,

154

picking up his primitive telephone. "An intruder has broken into my laboratory," he yelled into the receiver. "Please send someone over right away."

"Have it your way," Quadrel said with a grin as he backed out the door. "I don't need you anyway, Edison. I'll go into business myself. I've got ten thousand bucks. It doesn't buy much in 2001, but I'll be able to live like a king in 1879. And I'll make millions more inventing machines before their *real* inventors are even born! Hahaha!"

"You're a madman!" Edison said.

"No, I'm a genius," Quadrel said, "like you. Well, I better be going. It was a pleasure to meet you, Mr. Edison."

"You won't get far, sleazeball!" Barbara hollered.

Quadrel paused before leaving. "Oh, by the way, kids," he said. "Everybody back in the twenty-first century is really worried about you. Good luck finding your way back home!"

Then he let out a cackle and ran out the door.

With no immediate solution to their problem, Edison took Barbara and Qwerty home with him at the end of the day. The half-mile horse-and-buggy ride from the laboratory to Edison's mansion didn't take long. The children nudged each other as they made the right turn into Llewellyn Park and saw the few houses that would still be standing more than a hundred years later.

It was obvious that Edison didn't spend much time at home. His wife came running out of the house and hugged him as though he were a sailor who had been away at sea. She was pretty, but sad looking, and much younger than Edison. Her name was Mary, but the inventor greeted her as "Popsie-Wopsie."

Two children came running out of the house too. Seven-year-old Marion was blond and perky. She clung to Edison like she didn't want to let him go. He patted her on the head awkwardly and called her Dot.

Naturally, his skinny little boy was called Dash, even though his real name was Tom Jr. Just three years old, he had no idea that his father was one of the most famous men in the world. Upstairs, baby William was already asleep for the night.

"Who are *they*?" Dot asked her dad, wrinkling up her nose.

"These are my young friends Qwerty and Barbara Stevens," Edison said. "They'll be joining us this evening."

Dot made a mean face. She didn't see her father much and didn't like the idea of sharing his attention with two other kids.

The house, clearly, was Mary Edison's laboratory. Everything was perfect, like a museum. Elegant furniture was carefully arranged. The floors were covered by bearskin rugs. Flowers were everywhere. Dainty curtains hung over the windows, many of which were made of colorful stained glass. Edison's lab was a big mess, but his home was spotless.

Mary Edison hinted that young ladies were expected to "dress" for dinner. She gave Barbara a white, frilly dress to change into.

Dinner was tense, but not because someone was mad at someone else. It was just that everybody was so *quiet*. Mary Edison didn't seem to share her husband's natural curiosity for things. Even if she did, she would have had to shout for Edison to hear her thin voice, and it wouldn't be polite to shout at the table.

Two servants ran around constantly, bringing out more platters and taking away the dirty dishes. As the sun disappeared the servants went from room to room, lighting gaslights. While everyone ate in silence, Barbara kept stealing looks at Qwerty and nudging him under the table, trying to make him laugh.

"How was work today, Thomas?" Mrs. Edison finally asked when dinner was nearly finished.

"Fine," grunted Edison.

"That's nice. Please pass the—"

"Fine?" Qwerty blurted out excitedly. "He invented the electric light! It's, like, the most amazing invention since some cave guy invented the wheel thousands of years ago!"

Mrs. Edison shot Qwerty a dirty look. "Speak not when others are speaking," she said sternly. Barbara kicked Qwerty under the table.

"What are you learning in school, Dot?" Barbara asked politely.

"I don't attend school," Dot replied. "Father doesn't believe I need to."

"I went to school for three months when I was a boy," Edison grunted. "And I'm sorry I wasted that much time there."

After dinner everyone went up to the "sitting room," where, Qwerty discovered, people gathered to *sit*. The room was dark and gloomy, lit only by weak gaslights. Edison sat in the corner reading a magazine called *Transactions of the American Institute of Electrical Engineers*. Mrs. Edison sat at a

table working quietly on a jigsaw puzzle. Tom Jr. sat drawing pictures. Dot sat in a chair curled up with a book—*Decline and Fall of the Roman Empire*. Qwerty sat around wondering what was on TV back home.

It didn't appear as though the children had any toys. At one point Edison put down his magazine and brought out a box of alarm clocks for Dot to play with. He took one apart and put it together again. Then he told Dot to try it. When she didn't show interest in that game, Edison went back to his reading. He didn't seem to know what to make of children.

After a while Mrs. Edison went to the piano, and everyone gathered around her. When she began to play, Edison, oddly, got down on his knees and put his mouth on the edge of the keyboard.

"Why is your dad trying to eat the piano?" Qwerty whispered to Dot.

"Father can only hear the sound if it vibrates off the bones of his skull," she explained.

As Mrs. Edison played a jaunty version of "Camptown Races" there was a knock at the door.

One of the servants answered it. Two well-dressed young men stood in the hallway. One was Francis Upton, the man who had given Barbara the flowers earlier in the day and whom Edison had nicknamed Culture. Upton introduced his friend Jimmy Naismith, who was visiting from Massachusetts.

Upton gave Barbara more flowers and asked if she would sit on the front porch with him. She accepted the offer. It had to be better than sitting around the sitting room, Qwerty thought.

While Barbara and Upton went out on the porch, Jimmy Naismith chatted with the Edisons. He told them he was planning to study physical education at McGill University in Montreal.

"You need to go to college to learn how to *exercise*?" Edison snorted.

"I believe it is just as important to exercise the body as it is to exercise the mind," Naismith said. "Don't you agree, Mr. Edison?"

"The body is merely a container to carry your brain around in," Edison harumphed. "The only reason to exercise is if you don't *have* a brain."

Naismith looked like he'd been hit in the head with a brick.

Dot and Dash began yawning, and Mrs. Edison took them upstairs to bed. Qwerty wasn't tired, but there didn't seem to be anything worth staying up for either.

"I wish I had my Nintendo," he mumbled to himself.

"Speak up!" Edison barked.

"I said I intend to . . . get a breath of fresh air," Qwerty roared.

"I'll join you," Naismith said, realizing that if he didn't, he would be left alone with Edison.

Qwerty and Naismith went out the back door. A full moon lit up the sky. The Edison mansion had a huge yard, nearly the size of a football field. There was a big vegetable garden and a small building full of garden tools.

"Is there someplace around here we can shoot hoops?" Qwerty asked.

"Hoops?" Naismith replied. "What are hoops? Some type of bird? I don't believe in shooting animals."

"Hoops, *you* know," Qwerty said, pretending to take a jump shot.

The puzzled look on Naismith's face made Qwerty realize his favorite sport didn't exist in 1879.

"It's a cool game," he explained, picking up a big rubber ball that Edison's daughter must have left on the lawn. "There are two baskets at each end of the court, one for each team. You try to shoot the ball into the basket and prevent the other team from shooting it into yours. It's simple, really."

"Can you run with the ball like in football?" Naismith asked.

"No, no," Qwerty said, bouncing the rubber ball. "You dribble it, like this."

"Can you tackle the other fellows?" Naismith asked.

"That's a foul," Qwerty explained.

There were a bunch of bushel baskets lying around the garden. Qwerty took two of them and placed them about fifty feet apart on the dirt path leading to the back of Edison's mansion.

"In a real game these would be ten feet off the

ground," Qwerty said. "But this will do for now. Try and stop me."

Naismith stripped off his jacket and placed it carefully on the ground. Qwerty dribbled toward the basket, turning around when he needed to place his body between Naismith and the ball. Naismith, older and much taller than Qwerty, backed up, his feet getting tangled as Qwerty dribbled left and right.

Five feet from the basket Qwerty faked to the right. Naismith went for the fake, and Qwerty quickly dribbled left and slammed the ball in the basket.

"In your face!" Qwerty yelled. "That's two points for me."

Qwerty flipped Naismith the ball and told him it was his turn. Naismith bounced the ball awkwardly with both hands, but Qwerty didn't call him for double dribble. He decided to let Naismith get off a shot, seeing as how it was his first time playing the game.

Naismith dribbled downcourt—if you could call it dribbling. Halfway to the basket Naismith stopped, set up, and shot. The ball sailed way over the basket, bouncing down the road and rolling down the hill beyond the Edison property. Qwerty ran to get it, followed by Naismith.

Suddenly, in the middle of a big, open field, Qwerty stopped and turned around.

"What's the matter?" Naismith asked.

"I remember this place," Qwerty said.

"You've been here before?"

"Yes," Qwerty replied. "I mean, I'm going to live in a house, right here, on this spot . . . someday. I hope."

"You're a strange boy, Qwerty Stevens."

On the front porch Francis Upton removed his jacket and lovingly wrapped it around Barbara to protect her from the evening chill.

"'Sometimes hath the brightest day a cloud,'" Upton said. "'And after summer evermore succeeds / Barren winter, with his wrathful nipping cold: / So cares and joys abound, as seasons fleet.'"

"I love poetry," Barbara said. "Did you make that up?"

"No, alas, Mr. William Shakespeare did."

"It's beautiful."

Barbara didn't want to tell Upton the truth about herself. Not yet, anyway. She told him that she and Qwerty were visiting the Edisons on their way to their home in Washington. Upton seemed to believe anything that came from Barbara's lips, staring into her eyes like a lost puppy. He told her he had been working for Edison for a year. He was from Massachusetts and had studied mathematics and physics at Princeton.

"Would I be too forward in asking if I might hold your hand?" Upton asked after they had talked for nearly an hour.

"I guess not," Barbara said, embarrassed.

"Hands soft as the flesh of a babe's to hold, and just as wondrous to behold."

"Shakespeare?" Barbara asked.

"No," Upton laughed. "I made that up myself, actually."

"You're not at all like the boys . . . back home," Barbara sighed.

"Oh? What are the boys back home like?"

"You know," Barbara laughed. "Jerks. Idiots. Pigs. Losers. Troublemakers."

"It is beyond my comprehension how any man could behave in a boorish manner when in the company of someone as beautiful as yourself."

"Mr. Upton!" Barbara blushed. "You are very sweet."

After a while Upton released Barbara's hand and rose from the seat.

"'Parting is such sweet sorrow,'" he whispered. "'That I shall say good night till it be morrow.'"

Barbara sighed as she handed Upton back his coat. Upton collected his friend Naismith from the back of the house, where Qwerty was showing him the finer points of dribbling behind the back.

Barbara watched as the horse and buggy drove the two young men away. A thought crossed her mind: If Edison couldn't figure out a way to get her and Qwerty home, it might not be so terrible.

CHAPTER 18
Stuck in Time

First thing the next morning a wagon pulled by horses arrived at the Edison Laboratory. Two policemen got out. The officers escorted Ashley Quadrel, in handcuffs, toward the front gate. Edison's buggy arrived at the same time.

"I'm innocent!" Quadrel raved. "I want a lawyer!"

"Do you know this man, Mr. Edison?" one policeman asked.

"Not personally. What is he accused of?"

"Counterfeiting," the officer explained. "They picked him up in New York City. He was trying to pass off thousands of dollars of these obviously fake bills. He claims you can explain everything."

Edison took one of the five-dollar bills and chuckled. "This is the worst counterfeiting job I've seen. Look, he put Abe Lincoln on a fiver instead of Andy Jackson!"

The cops fell all over themselves laughing as they passed the bills around.

"It's the money of the future, you dimwits!" Quadrel yelled. "Lincoln *will* be on the five-dollar bill someday!"

"That's the day they'll let you out of jail!" one of the cops hooted.

"You've got to believe me," Quadrel begged. "Mr. Edison invented a fantastic machine that can send people anywhere, to any time. I live in the twenty-first century. So do these two kids. They'll tell you I'm not lying."

"Son," the policeman asked Qwerty, "what's the story?"

"I don't know what this man is talking about," Qwerty lied.

"How about you, miss?"

"He's cuckoo," Barbara said.

"So"—the cop turned to Quadrel—"you claim you come from the future and this is real money from that time, is that right?"

"Yes!" Quadrel exclaimed. "I know what's going to happen. There's going to be a World War in 1914, and another one in 1939. There are going to be nuclear weapons that can wipe out entire cities. There's going to be a new kind of music called rock and roll—"

"And I suppose men are going to walk on the Moon too?"

"Yes!" Quadrel said excitedly. "In 1969."

The cops looked at Edison, who looked at Qwerty, who shook his head.

"This man is a raving lunatic," Edison told the cops. "Take him away, boys."

As the police wagon drove off, Edison let out a belly laugh. He was in a jolly mood. One of his lightbulbs had survived all night without blowing out.

EDISON'S LIGHT.

The Great Inventor's Triumph in Electric Illumination.

SUCCESS IN A COTTON THREAD.

It Makes a Light, Without Gas or Flame, Cheaper Than Oil.

TRANSFORMED IN THE FURNACE.

Complete Details of the Perfected Carbon Lamp.

FIFTEEN MONTHS OF TOIL.

Story of His Tireless Experiments with Lamps, Burners and Generators.

The Wizard's Byplay, with Bodily Pain and Gold "Tailings."

HISTORY OF ELECTRIC LIGHTING.

The newspapers were already crowing about his incredible achievement. He was so pleased that he gave the Insomnia Squad a rare day off.

Edison led Qwerty and Barbara to the front gate

173

of the laboratory. They were about to go inside, when another buggy pulled up. Francis Upton bounded out.

"Good morning!" he said cheerfully. "It's a lovely day to celebrate with a drive in the country. Would Miss Stevens care to join me?"

"Sure!" Barbara said, scampering away to hop into the buggy.

"I guess that leaves you and me," Edison said as he guided Qwerty into the lab. "Now that I know the lamp works, I need to invent everything that will work with it. Switches, fuses, meters, cables, generators. Let's you and I conduct some experiments, shall we?"

Qwerty stopped at the door of the lab. He had been patient while Edison was creating the first light-bulb, but now his patience had worn thin.

"Mr. Edison, you've got your bulb," he said, the anger rising up in him. "Now it's time to concentrate on *my* problem. Me and my sister are stuck here. Forever. We'll never see the twenty-first century again. We'll never . . . be born. This wouldn't have happened if it wasn't for you and your machine. I think you owe us."

"It will take time—" Edison tried to explain.

"I don't *have* time!" Qwerty shouted.

"Look," Edison said softly, "solutions to problems don't always come when you want them to. But I believe every problem has a solution. Until we find it, I'll try to give you and your sister a good life. I'll take care of you like you were my own children. That's the least I can do for you."

"I just want to go home," Qwerty said, his eyes welling up with tears.

"I know," Edison said. "I'm sorry."

CHAPTER 19

A Change in Plans

Francis Upton, with Barbara Stevens at his side, steered his buggy onto a dirt road around the corner from the Edison Laboratory. In minutes they were in the country, trotting past farms, meadows, and grazing cows.

Barbara shook her head in wonder. Someday, she knew, this part of New Jersey would be covered with run-down cities, giant gas tanks, and Route 280, a superhighway that would stretch from Kearny to Lake Hiawatha. But looking around, she felt like she was in paradise.

"Tell me about yourself," Upton said, once he had stopped the buggy and spread a blanket under a shady tree for them to sit on.

"What do you want to know?" Barbara asked, a hint of nervousness in her voice. She had not spoken much of herself for fear of letting it slip that she came from the future.

"Tell me everything," Upton said. "What are your parents like?"

"My mom is a librarian. My father died almost seven years ago."

"I'm sorry."

"It was . . ."—Barbara was about to tell Upton that her father's car had been crushed by a drunk driver, but she realized the automobile hadn't even been invented yet—"an accident."

"It must have been very painful."

"I don't want to be a downer," Barbara said, struggling to change the subject.

"Downer?" Upton asked.

"You know, depressing. A bummer. Like this one time my little sister, Madison, was telling us her problems. She's usually pretty cool, but—"

"Cool?"

"Neat. Hip. With it. Anyway, Qwerty started torturing her and—"

"He tortured her?"

"Well, he was bugging her. And she started getting on his case—"

"His case?"

"Insulting him and stuff. So our mom grounded both of them—"

"Grounded?"

"Made them stay in the house, and—"

"You slay me, Miss Stevens!" Upton threw back his head and laughed. "Your use of the language is so unique, so innovative. I could listen to you talk all day."

"You really think so?"

"Miss Stevens, remember when you told me that I wasn't like the boys back home?"

"Yes."

"Well, you're not like the girls here either."

"Oh?" Barbara asked. "What are the girls here like?"

"You know," Upton replied. "Jerks. Idiots. Pigs. Losers. Troublemakers."

Both of them giggled uncontrollably. Barbara's head fell against his firm shoulder, and she kept it there.

"Francis," she said softly. "I don't want to go home. I want to stay here. With you."

Upton stopped and looked at Barbara.

"I will make you happier than Romeo made Juliet," he said softly.

"Will you do something for me?" Barbara asked.

"Anything."

"Let's go back to the lab."

Upton threw the blanket back in the buggy and headed for West Orange. When they pulled up to the gate, Barbara took Upton by the hand. She led him directly to Edison's secret hiding place. Nobody was there. The Anytime Anywhere Machine was sitting on the desk.

"We have to get rid of this," Barbara said.

"Why?" Upton asked. "What is it?"

"Trust me. It's a very bad invention."

"But Mr. Edison would never create an invention that was evil."

"He didn't mean to," Barbara said. "It just turned out that way."

"But I cannot just take it. It belongs to Mr. Edison, and anything Mr. Edison creates belongs, ultimately, to the world."

"Trust me, Francis. The world isn't ready for this. I'm not sure it ever will be. Do this for me, please."

Upton looked at the Anytime Anywhere Machine and then at Barbara.

"I will do almost anything for Mr. Edison," Upton said solemnly. "But I will do *absolutely* anything for you."

Upton removed the wires that attached the Anytime Anywhere Machine to the telegraph key. Barbara rummaged around in a closet until she found a wooden phonograph box that was large enough to fit the machine. Before locking the box, Upton took a sheet of paper out of Edison's desk and wrote on it:

From the Laboratory
of Thomas A. Edison,
Orange, N.J.

The world is not ready for this.
I'm not sure it ever will be.

October 1879

Barbara put the note in the box and clicked the lock shut.

"Let's go," she said.

"Where?"

"To Edison's house."

They walked out of the lab as quickly as they could without arousing suspicion. At the front gate Upton explained to the security guard that he was taking a phonograph home to repair it. The guard waved them through the gate, and they got into Upton's buggy.

"What are we going to do with it?" Upton asked

as he made the right turn into Llewellyn Park.

"You'll see," Barbara said. "Where can we get a shovel?"

Upton had one in the buggy's storage compartment. Barbara directed him to park down the road from Edison's mansion. She looked around, selected a spot, and began to dig.

Unaccustomed to seeing a lady doing manual labor, Upton took the shovel from Barbara and continued digging. When the hole was deep enough, Barbara lowered the box into it. Together they covered the hole with dirt and smoothed it over.

"What power do women exert," Upton said, "to make men wallow in the dirt?" He clapped the mud off his hands and wiped his forehead with a handkerchief.

"Is that Shakespeare?" Barbara asked.

"No, Upton."

Barbara brought her face close to his, closed her eyes, and hoped he would kiss her.

CHAPTER 20

The Key to Escape

Despite a two-day nationwide manhunt, investigators failed to find a single clue related to the disappearance of Qwerty and Barbara Stevens. Mrs. Stevens had begun to lose hope that she would ever see them again. She tried to be strong for Madison, but it was all she could do to make it through each day.

It was just as difficult for Madison Stevens. She missed her brother and sister terribly. It was lonely in the house without them. She missed the attention of her big sister, whom she idolized. She even missed Qwerty's constant teasing.

But in some small way she had to admit that she *liked* being the only child for a few days. She got all of her mother's attention. She didn't have to fight her way into the bathroom in the morning. Nobody messed with her toys.

All in all, though, she wished somebody would find her brother and sister.

Mrs. Stevens was preparing dinner when Madison went upstairs to play. On the way to her room she paused in front of Qwerty's door for a moment.

Madison turned the doorknob to see if it was locked. It wasn't. She went inside.

The Qwerty Museum, Madison called it. Clothes scattered around. Drawers open. Audio, video, and computer junk spilling out of boxes. If Qwerty didn't know where to put something, he would just dump it in the middle of the floor.

The computer was still on. If Qwerty and Barbara were never found, Madison thought, maybe she would get to keep their computer. It was a mean thought, she knew, but she thought it all the same. There were a few computers in her first-grade class, but Madison hadn't had her turn to use them yet.

She sat down at Qwerty's desk. Flying toasters moved relentlessly across the screen. Madison knew what a screen saver was, but she didn't know how to get it off the screen. She had asked Qwerty many times if he would teach her, but he always said she was too little to fool with the computer.

When she touched the mouse, the screen saver left the screen automatically. It was replaced by the Edison National Historic Site's Web page. Madison had just begun learning how to read, so the words didn't mean much to her. She had heard of Thomas Edison, but only because Qwerty's school was named after him.

Madison noticed that when she moved the mouse on the desk, a little pointer moved on the screen. She moved the pointer up and down, left and right. When nothing changed, she took her hand off the mouse. She didn't notice the button on the mouse, so she didn't click it.

She looked on the keyboard for the letters of her name and tapped the keys M-A-D-I-S-O-N. She expected to see her name on the screen, but it wasn't there. She tapped the big space bar a few times. Nothing happened.

She tapped the RETURN key.

Nothing happened.

She tapped the DELETE key.

Nothing happened.

And then she tapped the ESCAPE key.

At that instant, Qwerty was in the machine shop at the Edison Laboratory, washing out a bottle. Barbara was in the field behind Thomas Edison's house, about to kiss Francis Upton. Ashley Quadrel was in New York City, about to be locked in a jail cell.

When Madison tapped the ESCAPE key, Qwerty, Barbara, and Quadrel suddenly appeared in Qwerty's room with Madison.

"Eeeeeeeeeeeeek!" Madison screamed.

"Madison!" Qwerty and Barbara shouted.

While the Stevens children hugged each other joyfully, Ashley Quadrel dashed over to the window, climbed out, slid down the drainpipe, and ran away.

From the kitchen Mrs. Stevens heard Madison's scream and was up the stairs in seconds. "Madison!" she shouted as she reached the second floor. "Are you all right?"

That was when she saw Qwerty and Barbara and Madison hugging each other. Mrs. Stevens, overcome with emotion, dropped to her knees. The three children wrapped themselves around her.

For once Mrs. Stevens didn't care where Qwerty and Barbara had been or why they had left without permission. The only thing she cared about was that they were back.

"What's this hole in your T-shirt?" she asked Qwerty as they hugged.

"It's a long story, Mom."

CHAPTER 21

A Raving Lunatic

For centuries, researchers had been looking for proof that ESP, life after death, time travel, and other paranormal phenomena truly existed. *Now I've got that proof,* Ashley Quadrel thought as he dashed from the Stevenses' house. He was living proof! He had traveled back more than a century and returned safely. In his mind the achievement was equivalent to landing a man on the moon. He hurried to the offices of the Sixth Sense Institute to deliver the good news.

"Mr. Quadrel, you're under arrest," the policeman stationed outside the building said as he slapped handcuffs on him. "You have the right to remain silent—"

"Again?" Quadrel protested. "Listen, I have an important message to deliver."

The executives of the Sixth Sense Institute were summoned to the front of the building. Ashley Quadrel had already been read his rights, searched, and booked.

"This is a big misunderstanding," he claimed when the executives arrived. "Guys, I found the Anytime Anywhere Machine! It really works! I went back to 1879 with it."

"Yeah, sure," the president of Sixth Sense said. "Where's the ten thousand dollars you took from the safe?"

"I just borrowed it," Quadrel said. "I brought it with me when I went back to the past. The police there confiscated it because it didn't match the money they had back then. The important thing is, time travel is possible. Knowing that is worth more than ten thousand lousy bucks."

"You expect us to believe that ridiculous story?"

"You believe in *ghosts*!" Quadrel shouted. "You believed that guy in Utah who said he could bend spoons just by looking at them! You believe Bigfoot exists! Why don't you believe *me*?"

"Bigfoot never stole ten thousand bucks from our safe," the president of Sixth Sense said. "Take him away, officer."

Quadrel was dragged away, raving the whole time about those missing kids in West Orange, a box buried in the ground, computer scanners, and Thomas Edison. It would be a long time before he would be allowed back on the streets again.

CHAPTER 22

A Different Route

Ten minutes after Madison hit the ESCAPE key to bring her brother and sister back home, the Stevens family were still shouting their heads off in celebration. A car pulled into the driveway and a man got out.

"What's all the hubbub?" he asked as he came up the front steps.

The sight of Qwerty and Barbara caused him to start sobbing, run to them, and hug them furiously. Barbara's jaw dropped open, then she began blubbering uncontrollably.

"Who is this guy?" Qwerty whispered to Madison.

"It's Daddy, silly!" she giggled.

Daddy? Qwerty remembered his father, but not very well. The man *did* look a lot like the way he remembered. But Qwerty was sure his dad had died six years earlier. He had *seen* the body at the funeral. This guy had to be an imposter or something.

"Where have you been the last three days?" the man sobbed. "Mom and I have been so worried."

"We're back now," Barbara said, crying and laughing at the same time. "That's all that counts."

"Is he really Dad?" Qwerty whispered to Barbara.

"Yeah," she said, wiping tears away. "Something must have happened when we went back to 1879. We must have done something to alter history. Somehow we prevented the accident."

"But how? I didn't do anything," Qwerty insisted.

"Neither did I."

Qwerty's bewildered expression and less-than-enthusiastic hug made Mr. Stevens back off to give him some space.

"Are you okay, son?" Mr. Stevens asked.

"You . . . were hit by a car," Qwerty stammered. "And killed. At the corner of Franklin Avenue and Ridge Road. . . ."

"You must have had a bad dream," Mrs. Stevens said, trying to comfort Qwerty. "Daddy's right here."

"Franklin and Ridge?" Mr. Stevens said. "You can't drive there. That's where Naismith Park is, the one with all those basketball courts."

Qwerty didn't remember any park at that corner. "*Naismith* Park?" Qwerty suddenly felt woozy. "How long has it been there?"

"It was there when I was a boy," Mr. Stevens replied. "Grandpa, too. My grandfather told me they built Naismith Park around the time of World War I. He remembered because the guy who invented basketball, Naismith himself, donated a bunch of money and even came to West Orange for the dedication."

"*James* Naismith?" Qwerty asked.

"Yeah, that's the fellow. He was a gym teacher in

Massachusetts. They say he invented the game by nailing a couple of peach baskets on the walls of a YMCA. Can't imagine why he came all the way down to West Orange to build a park."

I can, Qwerty thought. If he hadn't given Naismith the idea for basketball in West Orange back in 1879, Naismith never would have come back to town and dedicated the park at the corner of Franklin and Ridge. And if there hadn't been a park at that inter-section, Qwerty's dad would have been driving through it on the night he was killed. But because of Naismith Park he took a different route and never had his accident.

And never died.

Qwerty's head was spinning. Barbara wrapped her arms around him. "Don't try to figure it all out," she whispered in his ear. "We're home. Dad's home. Just enjoy it."

Mr. and Mrs. Stevens hugged each other affection-ately. Madison, who could not tolerate her parents sharing a hug unless she was in on it, skipped over to them and joined in. Barbara, who enjoyed a good hug as much as anyone, squeezed in on the action too. Qwerty, who usually considered hugging to be a form of torture, wrapped his arms around everyone, causing them to topple over in a tangled mass of arms and legs and giggles.

For the first time in a long time home seemed like a pretty good place to be.

I think of this book as a plausible fantasy. I tried to blend fact and fiction to write an entertaining story that would also make the great inventor Thomas Edison come to life. Many of the names, places, and facts in this novel are true. The photos and patent drawings are real. Edison's wife and children, and the members of the Insomnia Squad were real people.

I learned a lot about Edison by visiting the Edison National Historic Site and reading *Edison: Inventing the Century*, by Neil Baldwin; *A Streak of Luck: The Life and Legend of Thomas Alva Edison*, by Robert Conot; *Edison: A Biography*, by Matthew Josephson; and *Edison*, by Rex Beasley. Much of

Edison's personality and even some of his dialogue came directly from *The Diary and Sundry Observations of Thomas Alva Edison.*

There are also a few whoppers in here:

• Edison *did* invent the electric light in 1879, but that was eight years *before* he built his laboratory in West Orange, New Jersey. He was working at Menlo Park, New Jersey, in 1879. I changed the location because Edison's home and lab in West Orange are still standing today, while little evidence of Edison is left in Menlo Park.

• Although Thomas and Mary Edison *did* live with their children (Dot, Dash, and baby William) in 1879, Mary never lived in West Orange. Tragically, she took ill and died five years after Edison invented the electric light. She was just twenty-nine. Edison's second wife, Mina, lived with him in West Orange for the rest of his life. Edison fathered six children altogether, three with each of his wives. But he was hopelessly devoted to his work, and family life was not very important to him.

• The description of how Edison invented the electric light is vastly simplified. In fact, the search for a filament was only a small part of what Edison had to do to put together an entire lighting system. However, the first successful filament *was* a simple cotton thread. Later Edison found cardboard worked even better. Today the filaments in your lightbulbs at home are made of tungsten, a metal that has a very high melting point.

Other tidbits:

• The newspaper article announcing Edison's success actually appeared in the *New York Herald* two months later. News traveled more slowly in those days.

• The Edison National Historic Site *does* have a Web site, but the time line is not interactive and does not include entries for every year of Edison's life.

• Edison's talking dolls didn't reach the market until 1890, and both men and women assembled them.

• Edison *did* write of his desire to create a machine that would make it possible to communicate with the dead, but he never built one.

• James Naismith really *was* a gym teacher who invented basketball by nailing peach baskets up in the YMCA Training School in Springfield, Massachusetts, in 1891. He was eighteen years old in 1879, but he never visited the home of Thomas Edison.

• The Stevenses, Ashley Quadrel, and all other present-day characters are fictional.

• If you don't know Spanish, the two sentences on pages 30 and 31 mean "I would like to take waterskiing lessons" and "The garbage has not been collected for three days."

• The word *ahoy* was used as a greeting when the telephone was first invented. In fact, some books credit Thomas Edison with inventing the word *hello*.

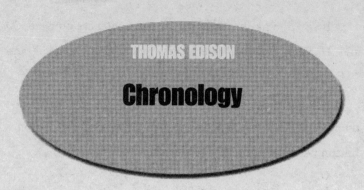

Chronology

1847: Is born February 11 in Milan, Ohio

1869: Declares himself an inventor; moves to New York City; is awarded his first patent, a vote recorder

1871: Mother dies; marries Mary Stilwell; sets up laboratory in Newark, New Jersey

1873: First child, Marion, born; begins work on quadruplex telegraph

1875: Invents mimeograph

1876: Constructs laboratory in Menlo Park, New Jersey; Tom Jr. born

1877: Invents phonograph

1878: Begins work on incandescent light; William born

1879: Begins work separating iron ore from stone

1880: Begins work on electric railroad

1881: Moves operations to Manhattan

1882: Applies for 141 patents, an average of one invention every two and a half days

1883: Discovers "the Edison effect," laying the basis for the radio tube

1884: Mary Stilwell Edison dies at age twenty-nine

1886: Marries Mina Miller; moves to West Orange, New Jersey

1887: Constructs laboratory in West Orange

1888: Madeleine born; improved phonograph introduced

1890: Talking doll introduced; Charles born

1893: Builds the first movie studio, in West Orange

1894: Kinetoscope parlor opens in New York City

1898: Theodore born

1899: Begins work on storage battery for electric cars

1903: First film with a plot, *The Great Train Robbery*, premieres

1911: Edison disc phonograph introduced

1926: Announces retirement at age eighty; son Charles will take over business

1927: Begins work extracting rubber from plants

1928: Is awarded Congressional Gold Medal

1931: Dies October 18 in West Orange, New Jersey